GRENDEL

JOHN GARDNER

Illustrated by
Emil Antonucci

VINTAGE BOOKS
A DIVISION OF RANDOM HOUSE
NEW YORK

First Vintage Books Edition, October 1985

Library of Congress Cataloging in Publication Data

Gardner, John, 1933–
   Grendel.

   I. Title.
PS3557.A712G7   1985   813'.54   85-40133
ISBN 0-394-74056-4 (pbk.)

Manufactured in the United States of America

For Joel and Lucy

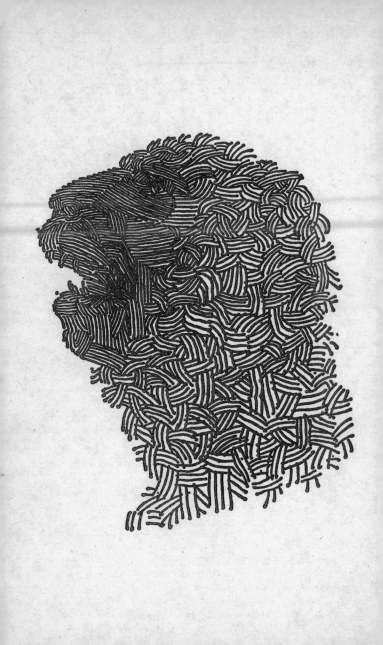

And if the Babe is born a Boy
He's given to a Woman Old,
Who nails him down upon a rock,
Catches his shrieks in cups of gold.
—WILLIAM BLAKE

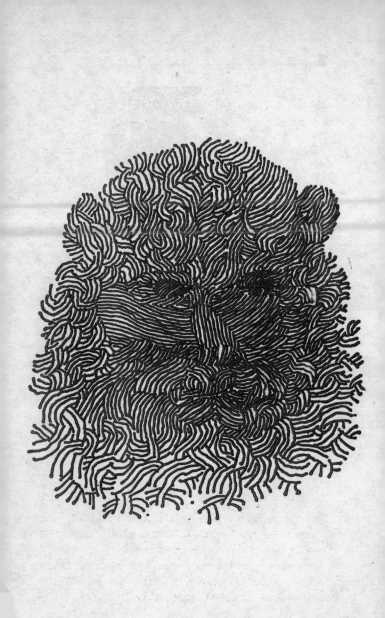

The old ram stands looking down over rockslides, stupidly triumphant. I blink. I stare in horror. "Scat!" I hiss. "Go back to your cave, go back to your cowshed—whatever." He cocks his head like an elderly, slow-witted king, considers the angles, decides to ignore me. I stamp. I hammer the ground with my fists. I hurl a skull-size stone at him. He will not budge. I shake my two hairy fists at the sky and I let out a howl so unspeakable that the water at my feet turns sudden ice and even I myself am left uneasy. But the ram stays; the season is upon us. And so begins the twelfth year of my idiotic war.

The pain of it! The stupidity!

"Ah, well," I sigh, and shrug, trudge back to the trees.

Do not think my brains are squeezed shut, like the ram's, by the roots of horns. Flanks atremble, eyes like stones, he stares at as much of the world as he can see and feels it surging in him, filling his chest as the melting snow fills dried-out creek-beds, tickling his gross, lopsided balls and charging his brains with the same unrest that made him suffer last year at this time, and the year before, and the year before that. (He's forgotten them all.) His hindparts shiver with the usual joyful, mindless ache to mount whatever happens near—the storm piling up black towers to the west, some rotting, docile stump, some spraddle-legged ewe. I cannot bear to look. "Why can't these creatures discover a little dignity?" I ask the sky. The sky says nothing, predictably. I make a face, uplift a defiant middle finger, and give an obscene little kick. The sky ignores me, forever unimpressed. Him too I hate, the same as I hate these brainless budding trees, these brattling birds.

Not, of course, that I fool myself with thoughts that I'm more noble. Pointless, ridiculous monster crouched in the shadows, stinking of dead men, murdered children, martyred cows. (I am neither proud nor ashamed, understand. One more dull victim, leering at seasons that never were meant to be observed.) "Ah, sad one, poor old freak!" I cry, and hug myself, and laugh, letting out salt tears, he he! till I fall down gasping and sobbing. (It's mostly fake.) The sun spins mindlessly overhead, the shadows lengthen and shorten as if by plan. Small birds, with a high-pitched yelp, lay eggs. The tender grasses peek up, innocent yellow, through the ground: the children of the dead. (It was just here, this shocking green, that once when the moon was tombed in clouds, I tore off sly old Athelgard's head. Here, where the startling tiny jaws of crocuses snap at the late-winter sun like the heads of baby watersnakes, here I killed the old woman with the irongray hair. She tasted of urine and spleen, which made me spit. Sweet mulch for yellow blooms. Such are the tiresome memories of a shadow-shooter, earth-rim-roamer, walker of the world's weird wall.) "Waaah!" I cry, with another quick, nasty face at the sky, mournfully observing the way it is, bitterly remembering the way it was, and idiotically casting tomorrow's nets. "Aargh! Yaww!" I reel, smash trees. Disfigured son of lunatics. The big-boled oaks gaze down at me yellow with morning, beneath complexity. "No offense," I say, with a terrible, sycophantish smile, and tip an imaginary hat.

It was not always like this, of course. On occasion it's been worse.

No matter, no matter.

The doe in the clearing goes stiff at sight of my horridness, then remembers her legs and is gone. It makes me cross. "Blind prejudice!" I bawl at the splintered sunlight where half a second ago she stood. I wring my fingers, put on a long face. "Ah, the unfairness of everything," I say, and shake my head. It is a matter of fact that I have never killed a deer in all my life, and never will. Cows have more meat and, locked up in pens, are easier to catch. It is true, perhaps, that I feel some trifling dislike of deer, but no more dislike than I feel for other natural things—discounting men. But deer, like rabbits and bears and even men, can make, concerning my race, no delicate distinctions. That is their happiness: they see all life without observing it. They're buried in it like crabs in mud. Except men, of course. I am not in a mood, just yet, to talk of men.

So it goes with me day by day and age by age, I tell myself. Locked in the deadly progression of moon and stars. I shake my head, muttering darkly on shaded paths, holding conversation with the only friend and comfort this world affords, my shadow.

Wild pigs clatter away through brush. A baby bird falls feet-up in my path, squeaking. With a crabby laugh, I let him lie, kind heaven's merciful bounty to some sick fox. So it goes with me, age by age. (Talking, talking. Spinning a web of words, pale walls of dreams, between myself and all I see.)

The first grim stirrings of springtime come (as I knew they must, having seen the ram), and even under the ground where I live, where no light breaks but the red of my fires and nothing stirs but the flickering shadows on my wet rock walls, or scampering rats on my piles of bones, or my mother's fat, foul bulk rolling over, restless again— molested by nightmares, old memories—I am aware in my chest of tuberstirrings in the blacksweet duff of the forest overhead. I feel my anger coming back, building up like invisible fire, and at last, when my soul can no longer resist, I go up—as mechanical as anything else—fists clenched against my lack of will, my belly growling, mindless as wind, for blood. I swim up through the firesnakes, hot dark whalecocks prowling the luminous green of the mere, and I surface with a gulp among churning waves and smoke. I crawl up onto the bank and catch my breath.

It's good at first to be out in the night, naked to the cold mechanics of the stars. Space hurls outward, falconswift, mounting like an irreversible injustice, a final disease. The cold night air is reality at last: indifferent to me as a stone face carved on a high cliff wall to show that the world is abandoned. So childhood too feels good at first, before one happens to notice the terrible sameness, age after age. I lie there resting in the steaming grass, the old lake hissing and gurgling behind me, whispering patterns of words my sanity resists. At last, heavy as an ice-capped mountain, I rise and work my way to the inner wall, beginning of wolfslopes, the edge of my realm. I stand in the high wind balanced, blackening the night with my stench, gazing down to cliffs that fall away to cliffs, and once again I am aware of my potential: I could die. I cackle with rage and suck in breath.

"Dark chasms!" I scream from the cliff-edge, "seize me! Seize me to your foul black bowels and crush my bones!" I am terrified at the sound of my own huge voice in the darkness. I stand there shaking from head to foot, moved to the deep-sea depths of my being, like a creature thrown into audience with thunder.

At the same time, I am secretly unfooled. The uproar is only my own shriek, and chasms are, like all things vast, inanimate. They will not snatch me in a thousand years, unless, in a lunatic fit of religion, I jump.

I sigh, depressed, and grind my teeth. I toy with shouting some tidbit more—some terrifying, unthinkable threat, some blackly fuliginous riddling hex—but my heart's not in it. "Missed me!" I say with a coy little jerk and a leer, to keep my spirits up. Then, with a sigh, a kind of moan, I start very carefully down the cliffs that lead to the fens and moors and Hrothgar's hall. Owls cross my path as silently as raiding ships, and at the sound of my foot, lean wolves rise, glance at me awkwardly, and, neat of step as lizards, sneak away. I used to take some pride in that—the caution of owls when my shape looms in, the alarm I stir in these giant northern wolves. I was younger then. Still playing cat and mouse with the universe.

I move down through the darkness, burning with murderous lust, my brains raging at the sickness I

can observe in myself as objectively as might a
mind ten centuries away. Stars, spattered out
through lifeless night from end to end, like jewels
scattered in a dead king's grave, tease, torment my
wits toward meaningful patterns that do not exist.
I can see for miles from these rock walls: thick
forest suddenly still at my coming—cowering stags,
wolves, hedgehogs, boars, submerged in their
stifling, unmemorable fear; mute birds, pulsating,
thoughtless clay in hushed old trees, thick limbs
interlocked to seal drab secrets in.

I sigh, sink into the silence, and cross it like
wind. Behind my back, at the world's end, my pale
slightly glowing fat mother sleeps on, old, sick at
heart, in our dingy underground room. Life-bloated,
baffled, long-suffering hag. Guilty, she imagines, of
some unremembered, perhaps ancestral crime.
(She must have some human in her.) Not that she
thinks. Not that she dissects and ponders the dusty
mechanical bits of her miserable life's curse. She
clutches at me in her sleep as if to crush me. I
break away. "Why are we here?" I used to ask
her. "Why do we stand this putrid, stinking hole?"
She trembles at my words. Her fat lips shake.
"Don't ask!" her wiggling claws implore. (She
never speaks.) "Don't ask!" It must be some terrible
secret, I used to think. I'd give her a crafty squint.
She'll tell me, in time, I thought. But she told me
nothing. I waited on. That was before the old dragon, calm as winter, unveiled the truth. He was not a
friend.

And so I come through trees and towns to the
lights of Hrothgar's meadhall. I am no stranger here.
A respected guest. Eleven years now and going on
twelve I have come up this clean-mown central hill,
dark shadow out of the woods below, and have

knocked politely on the high oak door, bursting its hinges and sending the shock of my greeting inward like a cold blast out of a cave. "Grendel!" they squeak, and I smile like exploding spring. The old Shaper, a man I cannot help but admire, goes out the back window with his harp at a single bound, though blind as a bat. The drunkest of Hrothgar's thanes come reeling and clanking down from their wall-hung beds, all shouting their meady, outrageous boasts, their heavy swords aswirl like eagles' wings. "Woe, woe, woe!" cries Hrothgar, hoary with winters, peeking in, wide-eyed, from his bedroom in back. His wife, looking in behind him, makes a scene. The thanes in the meadhall blow out the lights and cover the wide stone fieplace with shields. I laugh, crumple over; I can't help myself. In the darkness, I alone see clear as day. While they squeal and screech and bump into each other, I silently sack up my dead and withdraw to the woods. I eat and laugh and eat until I can barely walk, my chest-hair matted with dribbled blood, and then the roosters on the hill crow, and dawn comes over the roofs of the houses, and all at once I am filled with gloom again.

"This is some punishment sent us," I hear them bawling from the hill.

My head aches. Morning nails my eyes.

"Some god is angry," I hear a woman keen. "The people of Scyld and Herogar and Hrothgar are mired in sin!"

My belly rumbles, sick on their sour meat. I crawl through bloodstained leaves to the eaves of the forest, and there peak out. The dogs fall silent at the edge of my spell, and where the king's hall surmounts the town, the blind old Shaper, harp clutched tight to his fragile chest, stares futilely down, straight at me. Otherwise nothing. Pigs root dully at the posts of a wooden fence. A rumple-horned ox lies chewing in dew and shade. A few men, lean, wearing animal skins, look up at the gables of the king's hall, or at the vultures circling casually beyond. Hrothgar says nothing, hoarfrost-bearded, his features cracked and crazed. Inside, I hear the people praying—whimpering, whining, mumbling, pleading—to their numerous sticks and stones. He doesn't go in. The king has lofty theories of his own.

"Theories," I whisper to the bloodstained ground. So the dragon once spoke. ("They'd map out roads through Hell with their crackpot theories!" I recall his laugh.)

Then the groaning and praying stop, and on the side of the hill the dirge-slow shoveling begins. They throw up a mound for the funeral pyre, for whatever arms or legs or heads my haste has left behind. Meanwhile, up in the shattered hall, the builders are hammering, replacing the door for (it must be) the fiftieth or sixtieth time, industrious and witless as worker ants—except that they make small, foolish changes, adding a few more iron pegs, more iron bands, with tireless dogmatism.

Now fire. A few little lizard tongues, then healthy flames reaching up through the tangled nest of sticks. (A feeble-minded crow could have fashioned a neater nest.) A severed leg swells up and bursts, then an arm, then another, and the red fire turns on the blackening flesh and makes it sizzle, and it reaches higher, up and up into greasy smoke, turning, turning like falcons at warplay, rushing like circling wolves up into the swallowing, in-different sky. And now, by some lunatic theory, they throw on golden rings, old swords, and braided helmets. They wail, the whole crowd, women and men, a kind of song, like a single quavering voice. The song rings up like the greasy smoke and their faces shine with sweat and something that looks like joy. The song swells, pushes through woods and sky, and they're singing now as if by some lunatic theory they had won. I shake with rage. The red sun blinds me, churns up my belly to nausea, and the heat thrown out of the bone-fire burns my skin. I cringe, clawing my flesh, and flee for home.

2

Talking, talking, spinning a spell, pale skin of words that closes me in like a coffin. Not in a language that anyone any longer understands. Rushing, degenerate mutter of noises I send out before me wherever I creep, like a dragon burning his way through vines and fog.

I used to play games when I was young—it might as well be a thousand years ago. Explored our far-flung underground world in an endless wargame of leaps onto nothing, ingenious twists into freedom or new perplexity, quick whispered plottings with invisible friends, wild cackles when vengeance was mine. I nosed out, in my childish games, every last shark-toothed chamber and hall, every black tentacle of my mother's cave, and so came at last, adventure by adventure, to the pool of fire-snakes. I stared, mouth gaping. They were gray as old ashes; faceless, eyeless. They spread the surface of the water with pure green flame. I knew—I seemed to have known all along—that the snakes were there to guard something. Inevitably, after I'd stood there a while, rolling my eyes back along the dark hallway, my ears cocked for my mother's step, I screwed my nerve up and dove. The firesnakes scattered as if my flesh were charmed. And so I discovered the sunken door, and so I came up, for the first time, to moonlight.

I went no farther, that first night. But I came out again, inevitably. I played my way farther out into the world, vast cavern aboveground, cautiously darting from tree to tree challenging the terrible forces of night on tiptoe. At dawn I fled back.

I lived those years, as do all young things, in a spell. Like a puppy nipping, playfully growling preparing for battle with wolves. At times the spell would be broken suddenly: on shelves or in hallways of my mother's cave, large old shapes with smouldering eyes sat watching me. A continuous grumble came out of their mouths; their backs were humped. Then little by little it dawned on me that the eyes that seemed to bore into my body were in fact gazing through it, wearily indifferent to my slight obstruction of the darkness. Of all the creatures I knew, in those days, only my mother really looked at me.—Stared at me as if to consume me, like a troll. She loved me, in some mysterious sense I understood without her speaking it. I was her creation. We were one thing, like the wall and the rock growing out from it.— Or so I ardently, desperately affirmed. When her strange eyes burned into me, it did not seem quite sure. I was intensely aware of where I sat, the volume of darkness I displaced, the shiny-smooth span of packed dirt between us, and the shocking separateness from me in my mama's eyes. I would feel, all at once, alone and ugly, almost—as if I'd dirtied myself—obscene. The cavern river rumbled far below us. Being young, unable to face these things, I would bawl and hurl myself at my mother and she would reach out her claws and seize me, though I could see I alarmed her (I had teeth like a saw), and she would smash me to her fat, limp breast as if to make me a part of her flesh again. After that, comforted, I would gradually ease back out into my games. Crafty-eyed, wicked as an elderly wolf, I would scheme with or stalk my imaginary friends, projecting the self I meant to become into every dark corner of the cave and the woods above.

Then all at once there they'd be again, the indifferent, burning eyes of the strangers. Or my mother's eyes. Again my world would be suddenly transformed, fixed like a rose with a nail through it, space hurtling coldly out from me in all directions. But I didn't understand.

One morning I caught my foot in the crack where two old treetrunks joined. "Owp!" I yelled. "Mama! Waa!" I was out much later than I'd meant to be. As a rule I was back in the cave by dawn, but that day I'd been lured out farther than usual by the heavenly scent of newborn calf—ah, sweeter than flowers, as sweet as my mama's milk. I looked at the foot in anger and disbelief. It was wedged deep, as if the two oak trees were eating it. Black sawdust—squirreldust—was spattered up the leg almost to the thigh. I'm not sure now how the accident happened. I must have pushed the two boles apart as I stepped up into the place where they joined, and then when I stupidly let go again they closed on my foot like a trap. Blood gushed from my ankle and shin, and pain flew up through me like fire up the flue of a mountain. I lost my head. I bellowed for help, so loudly it made the ground shake. "Mama! Waa! Waaa!" I bellowed to the sky, the forest, the cliffs, until I was so weak from loss of blood I could barely wave my arms. "I'm going to die," I wailed. "Poor Grendel! Poor old Mama!" I wept and sobbed. "Poor Grendel will hang here and starve to death," I told myself, "and no one will ever even miss him!" The thought enraged me. I hooted. I thought of my mother's foreign eyes, staring at me from across the room: I thought of the cool, indifferent eyes of the others. I shrieked in fear; still no one came.

The sun was up now, and even filtered as it was through the lacy young leaves, it made my head hurt. I twisted around as far as I could, hunting wildly for her shape on the cliffs, but there was nothing, or, rather, there was everything but my mother. Thing after thing tried, cynical and cruel, to foist itself off as my mama's shape—a black rock balanced at the edge of the cliff, a dead tree casting a long-armed shadow, a running stag, a cave entrance—each thing trying to detach itself, lift itself out of the general meaningless scramble of objects, but falling back, melting to the blank, infuriating clutter of not-my-mother. My heart began to race. I seemed to see the whole universe, even the sun and sky, leaping forward, then sinking away again, decomposing. Everything was wreckage, putrefaction. If she were there, the cliffs, the brightening sky, the trees, the stag, the waterfall would suddenly snap into position around her, sane again, well organized; but she was not, and the morning was crazy. Its green brilliance jabbed at me, live needles.

"Please, Mama!" I sobbed as if heartbroken.

Then, some thirty feet away, there was a bull. He stood looking at me with his head lowered, and the world snapped into position around him, as if in league with him. I must have been closer to the calf than I had guessed, since he'd arrived to protect it. Bulls do such things, though they don't even know that the calves they defend are theirs. He shook his horns at me, as if scornful. I trembled. On the ground, on two good feet, I would have been more than a match for the bull, or if not, I could have outrun him. But I was four or five feet up in the air, trapped and weak. He could slam me right out of the tree with one blow of that boned, square head, maybe tearing the foot off, and then he could gore me to death at his leisure in the grass. He pawed the ground, looking at me up-from-under, murderous. "Go away!" I said. "Hssst!" It had no effect. I bellowed at him. He jerked his head as if the sound were a boulder I'd thrown at him, but then he merely stood considering, and, after a minute, he pawed the ground again. Again I bellowed. This time he hardly noticed it. He snorted through his nose and pawed more deeply, spattering grass and black earth at his sharp rear hooves. As if time had slowed down as it does for the dying, I watched him loll his weight forward, sliding into an easy lope, head tilted, coming toward me in a casual arc. He picked up speed, throwing his weight onto his huge front shoulders, crooked tail lifted behind him like a flag. When I screamed, he didn't even flick an ear but came on, driving like an avalanche now, thunder booming from his hooves across the cliffs. The same instant he struck my tree he jerked his head and flame shot up my leg. The tip of one horn had torn me to the knee.

But that was all. The tree shuddered as he banged it with his skull, and he pivoted around it, stumbling. He gave his head a jerk, as if clearing his brains, then turned and loped back to where he'd charged me from before. He'd struck too low, and even in my terror I understood that he would always strike too low: he fought by instinct, blind mechanism ages old. He'd have fought the same way against an earthquake or an eagle: I had nothing to fear from his wrath but that twisting horn. The next time he charged I kept my eye on it, watched that horn with as much concentration as I'd have watched the rims of a crevasse I was leaping, and at just the right instant I flinched. Nothing touched me but the breeze as the horn flipped past.

I laughed. My ankle was numb now; my leg was on fire to the hip. I twisted to search the cliffwalls again, but still my mother wasn't there, and my laughter grew fierce. All at once, as if by sudden vision, I understood the emptiness in the eyes of those humpbacked shapes back in the cave. (Were they my brothers, my uncles, those creatures shuffling brimstone-eyed from room to room, or sitting separate, isolated, muttering forever like underground rivers, each in his private, inviolable gloom?)

I understood that the world was nothing: a mechanical chaos of casual, brute enmity on which we stupidly impose our hopes and fears. I understood that, finally and absolutely, I alone exist. All the rest, I saw, is merely what pushes me, or what I push against, blindly—as blindly as all that is not myself pushes back. I create the whole universe, blink by blink.—An ugly god pitifully dying in a tree!

The bull struck again. I flinched from the horn-tip and bellowed with rage and pain. The limbs overhead, stretching out through the clearing like hungry snakes reaching up from their nest, would be clubs if I had them in my two hands, or barricades, piled between me and my cave, or kindling down in the room where my mother and I slept. Where they were, above me, they were—what? Kind shade? I laughed. A tearful howl.

The bull kept on charging. Sometimes after he hit he'd fall down and lie panting. I grew limp with my anarchistic laughter. I no longer bothered to jerk back my leg. Sometimes the horntip tore it, sometimes not. I clung to the treetrunk that slanted off to my right, and I almost slept. Perhaps I did sleep, I don't know. I must have. Nothing mattered. Sometime in the middle of the afternoon I opened my eyes and discovered that the bull was gone.

I slept again, I think. When I woke up this time and looked up through the leaves overhead, there were vultures. I sighed, indifferent. I was growing used to the pain, or it had lessened. Unimportant. I tried to see myself from the vultures' viewpoint. I saw, instead, my mother's eyes. Consuming. I was suddenly her focus of the general meaninglessness —not for myself, not for any quality of my large, shaggy body or my sly, unnatural mind. I was, in her eyes, some meaning I myself could never know and might not care to know: an alien, the rock broken free of the wall. I slept again.

That night, for the first time, I saw men.

It was dark when I awakened—or when I came to, if it was that. I was aware at once that there was something wrong. There was no sound, not even the honk of a frog or the chirp of a cricket. There was a smell, a fire very different from ours, pungent, painful as thistles to the nose. I opened my eyes and everything was blurry, as though underwater. There were lights all around me, like some weird creature's eyes. They jerked back as I looked. Then voices, speaking words. The sounds foreign at first, but when I calmed myself, concentrating, I found I understood them: it was my own language, but spoken in a strange way, as if the sounds were made by brittle sticks, dried spindles, flaking bits of shale. My vision cleared and I saw them, mounted on horses, holding torches up. Some of them had shiny domes (as it seemed to me then) with horns coming out, like the bull's. They were small, these creatures, with dead-looking eyes and gray-white faces, and yet in some ways they were like us, except ridiculous and, at the same time, mysteriously irritating, like rats. Their movements were stiff and regular, as if figured by logic. They had skinny, naked hands that moved by clicks. When I first became aware of them, they were all speaking at the same time. I tried to move, but my body was rigid; only one hand gave a jerk. They all stopped speaking at the same instant, like sparrows. We stared at each other.

One of them said—a tall one with a long black beard—"It moves independent of the tree."

They nodded.

The tall one said, "It's a growth of some kind, that's my opinion. Some beastlike fungus."

They all looked up into the branches.

A short, fat one with a tangled white beard pointed up into the tree with an ax. "Those branches on the northern side are all dead there. No doubt the whole tree'll be dead before midsummer. It's always the north side goes first when there ain't enough sap."

They nodded, and another one said, "See there where it grows up out of the trunk? Sap running all over."

They leaned over the sides of their horses to look, pushing the torches toward me. The horses' eyes glittered.

"Have to close that up if we're going to save this tree," the tall one said. The others grunted, and the tall one looked up at my eyes, uneasy. I couldn't move. He stepped down off the horse and came over to me, so close I could have swung my hand and smashed his head if I could make my muscles move. "It's like blood," he said, and made a face.

Two of the others got down and came over to pull at their noses and look.

"I say that tree's a goner," one of them said.

They all nodded, except the tall one. "We can't just leave it rot," he said. "Start letting the place go to ruin and you know what the upshot'll be."

They nodded. The others got down off their horses and came over. The one with the tangled white beard said, "Maybe we could chop the fungus out."

They thought about it. After a while the tall one shook his head. "I don't know. Could be it's some kind of a oaktree spirit. Better not to mess with it."

They looked uneasy. There was a hairless, skinny one with eyes like two holes. He stood with his arms out, like a challenged bird, and he kept moving around in jerky little circles, bent forward, peering at everything, at the tree, at the woods around, up into my eyes. Now suddenly he nodded. "That's it! King's right! It's a spirit!"

"You think so?" they said. Their heads poked forward.

"Sure of it," he said.

"Is it friendly, you think?" the king said.

The hairless one peered up at me with the fingertips of on hand in his mouth. The skinny elbow hung straight down, as if he were leaning on an invisible table while he thought the whole thing through. His black little eyes stared straight into mine, as if waiting for me to tell him something. I tried to speak. My mouth moved, but nothing would come out. The little man jerked back. "He's hungry!" he said.

"Hungry!" they all said. "What does he eat?"

He looked at me again. His tiny eyes drilled into me and he was crouched as if he were thinking of trying to jump up into my brains. My heart thudded. I was so hungry I could eat a rock. He smiled suddenly, as if a holy vision had exploded in his head. "He eats *pig!*" he said. He looked doubtful. "Or maybe pigsmoke. He's in a period of transition."

They all looked at me, thinking it over, then nodded.

The king picked out six men. "Go get the thing some pigs," he said. The six men said "Yes sir!" and got on their horses and rode off. It filled me with joy, though it was all crazy, and before I knew I could do it, I laughed. They jerked away and stood shaking, looking up.

"The spirit's angry," one of them whispered.

"It always has been," another one said. "That's why it's killing the tree."

"No, no, you're wrong," the hairless one said. "It's yelling for pig."

"Pig!" I tried to yell. It scared them.

They all began shouting at each other. One of the horses neighed and reared up, and for some crazy reason they took it for a sign. The king snatched an ax from the man beside him and, without any warning, he hurled it at me. I twisted, letting out a howl, and it shot past my shoulder, just barely touching my skin. Blood trickled out.

"You're all crazy," I tried to yell, but it came out a moan. I bellowed for my mother.

"Surround him!" the king yelled, "Save the horses!"—and suddenly I knew I was dealing with no dull mechanical bull but with thinking creatures, pattern makers, the most dangerous things I'd ever met. I shrieked at them, trying to scare them off, but they merely ducked behind bushes and took long sticks from the saddles of their horses, bows and javelins. "You're all crazy," I bellowed, "you're all insane!" I'd never howled more loudly in my life. Darts like hot coals went through my legs and arms and I howled more loudly still. And then, just when I was sure I was finished, a shriek ten times as loud as mine came blaring off the cliff. It was my mother! She came roaring down like thunder, screaming like a thousand hurricanes, eyes as bright as dragonfire, and before she was within a mile of us, the creatures had leaped to their horses and galloped away. Big trees shattered and fell from her path; the earth trembled. Then her smell poured in like blood into a silver cup, filling the moonlit clearing to the brim, and I felt the two trees that held me falling, and I was tumbling, free, into the grass.

I woke up in the cave, warm firelight flickering on walls. My mother lay picking through the bone pile. When she heard me stir, she turned, wrinkling her forehead, and looked at me. There were no other shapes. I think I dimly understood even then that they'd gone deeper into darkness, away from men. I tried to tell her all that had happened, all that I'd come to understand: the meaningless objectness of the world, the universal bruteness. She only stared, troubled at my noise. She'd forgotten all language long ago, or maybe had never known any. I'd never heard her speak to the other shapes. (How I myself learned to speak I can't remember; it was a long, long time ago.) But I talked on, trying to smash through the walls of her unconsciousness. "The world resists me and I resist the world," I said. "That's all there is. The mountains are what I define them as." Ah, monstrous stupidity of childhood, unreasonable hope! I waken with a start and see it over again (in my cave, out walking, or sitting by the mere), the memory rising as if it has been pursuing me. The fire in my mother's eyes brightens and she reaches out as if some current is tearing us apart. "The world is all pointless accident," I say. Shouting now, my fists clenched. "I exist, nothing else." Her face works. She gets up on all fours, brushing dry bits of bone from her path, and, with a look of terror, rising as if by unnatural power, she hurls herself across the void and buries me in her bristly fur and fat. I sicken with fear. "My mother's fur is bristly," I say to myself. "Her flesh is loose." Buried under my mother I cannot see. She smells of wild pig and fish. "My mother smells of wild pig and fish," I say. What I see I inspire with usefulness, I think, trying to suck in breath, and all that I do not see is useless, void. I observe myself observing what I observe. It startles me. "Then I am not that which observes!" I am *lack. Alack!* No thread, no frailest hair between myself and the universal clutter! I listen to the underground river. I have never seen it.

Talking, talking, spinning a skin, a skin . . .

I can't breathe, and I claw to get free. She struggles. I smell my mama's blood and, alarmed, I hear from the walls and floor of the cave the booming, booming, of her heart.

3

It wasn't because he threw that battle-ax that I turned on Hrothgar. That was mere midnight foolishness. I dismissed it, thought of it afterward only as you remember a tree that fell on you or an adder you stepped on by accident, except of course that Hrothgar was more to be feared than a tree or snake. It wasn't until later, when I was full-grown and Hrothgar was an old, old man, that I settled my soul on destroying him—slowly and cruelly. Except for his thanes' occasional stories of seeing my footprints, he'd probably forgotten by then that I existed.

He'd been busy. I'd watched it all from the eaves of the forest, mostly from up off the ground, in the branches.

In the beginning there were various groups of them: ragged little bands that roamed the forest on foot or horseback, crafty-witted killers that worked in teams, hunting through the summer, shivering in caves or little huts in the winter, occasionally wandering out into the snow to plow through it slowly, clumsily, after more meat. Ice clung to their eyebrows and beards and eyelashes, and I'd hear them whining and groaning as they walked. When two hunters from different bands came together in the woods, they would fight until the snow was slushy with blood, then crawl back, gasping and crying, to their separate camps to tell wild tales of what happened.

As the bands grew larger, they would seize and clear a hill and, with the trees they'd cut, would set up shacks, and on the crown of the hill a large, shaggy house with a steeply pitched roof and a wide stone hearth, where they'd all go at night for protection from other bands of men. The inside walls would be beautifully painted and hung with tapestries, and every cross-timber or falcon's perch was carved and gewgawed with toads, snakes, dragon shapes, deer, cows, pigs, trees, trolls. At the first sign of spring they would set out their shrines and scatter seeds on the sides of the hill, below the shacks, and would put up wooden fences to pen their pigs and cows. The women worked the ground and milked and fed the animals while the men hunted, and when the men came in from the wolf-roads at dusk, the women would cook the game they'd caught while the men went inside and drank mead. Then they'd all eat, the men first, then the women and children, the men still drinking, getting louder and braver, talking about what they were going to do to the bands on the other hills. I would huddle, listening to their noise in the darkness, my eyebrows lifted, my lips pursed, the hair on the back of my neck standing up like pigs' bristles. All the bands did the same thing. In time I began to be more amused than revolted by what they threatened. It didn't matter to me what they did to each other. It was slightly ominous because of its strangeness—no wolf was so vicious to other wolves—but I half believed they weren't serious.

They would listen to each other at the mead-hall tables, their pinched, cunning rats' faces picking like needles at the boaster's words, the warfalcons gazing down, black, from the rafters, and when one of them finished his raving threats, another would stand up and lift up his ram's horn, or draw his sword, or sometimes both if he was very drunk, and he'd tell them what *he* planned to do. Now and then some trivial argument would break out, and one of them would kill another one, and all the others would detach themselves from the killer as neatly as blood clotting, and they'd consider the case and they'd either excuse him, for some reason, or else send him out to the forest to live by stealing from their outlying pens like a wounded fox. At times I would try to befriend the exile, at other times I would try to ignore him, but they were treacherous. In the end, I had to eat them. As a rule, though, that wasn't how all their drinking turned out. Normally the men would howl out their daring, and the evening would get merrier, louder and louder, the king praising this one, criticizing that one, no one getting hurt except maybe some female who was asking for it, and eventually they'd all fall asleep on each other like lizards, and I'd steal a cow.

But the threats were serious. Darting unseen from camp to camp, I observed a change come over their drunken boasts. It was late spring. Food was plentiful. Every sheep and goat had its wobbly twins, the forest was teeming, and the first crops of the hillsides were coming into fruit. A

man would roar, "I'll steal their gold and burn
their meadhall!" shaking his sword as if the tip
were afire, and a man with eyes like two pins
would say, "Do it now, Cowface! I think you're
not even the man your father was!" The people
would laugh. I would back away into the darkness, furious at my stupid need to spy on them,
and I would glide to the next camp of men, and
I'd hear the same.

Then once, around midnight, I came to a hall
in ruins. The cows in their pens lay burbling
blood through their nostrils, with javelin holes in
their necks. None had been eaten. The watchdogs
lay like dark wet stones, with their heads cut off,
teeth bared. The fallen hall was a square of
flames and acrid smoke, and the people inside
(none of them had been eaten either) were burned
black, small, like dwarfs turned dark and crisp.
The sky opened like a hole where the gables had
loomed before, and the wooden benches, the
trestle tables, the beds that had hung on the meadhall walls were scattered to the edge of the forest,
shining charcoal. There was no sign of the gold
they'd kept—not so much as a melted hilt.

Then the wars began, and the war songs, and
the weapon making. If the songs were true, as I
suppose at least one or two of them were, there
had always been wars, and what I'd seen was
merely a period of mutual exhaustion.

I'd been watching a meadhall from high in a
tree, night-birds singing in the limbs below me,
the moon's face hidden in a tower of clouds, and
nothing would be stirring except leaves moving
in the light spring breeze and, down by the pig-
pens, two men walking with their battle-axes and
their dogs. Inside the hall I would hear the Shaper

telling of the glorious deeds of dead kings—how they'd split certain heads, snuck away with certain precious swords and necklaces—his harp mimicking the rush of swords, clanging boldly with the noble speeches, sighing behind the heroes' dying words. Whenever he stopped, thinking up formulas for what to say next, the people would all shout and thump each other and drink to the Shaper's long life. In the shadow of the hall and by the outbuildings, men sat whistling or humming to themselves, repairing weapons: winding bronze bands around gray ashspears, treating their sword-blades with snake's venom, watching the gold-worker decorate the handles of battle-axes. (The goldworkers had an honored place. I remember one of them especially: a lean, aloof, superior man of middle age. He never spoke to the others except to laugh sometimes—"Nyeh heh heh.")

Then suddenly the birds below me in the tree would fall silent, and beyond the meadhall clearing I'd hear the creak of harness-leather. The watchmen and their dogs would stand stock-still, as if lightning-struck; then the dogs would bark, and the next instant the door would bang open and men would come tumbling, looking crazy, from the meadhall. The enemies' horses would thunder up into the clearing, leaping the pig-fences, sending the cows and the pigs away mooing and squealing, and the two bands of men would charge. Twenty feet apart they would slide to a stop and stand screaming at each other with raised swords. The leaders on both sides held their javelins high in both hands and shook them, howling their lungs out. Terrible threats, from the few words I could catch. Things about their fathers and their fathers' fathers, things about justice and honor and lawful revenge—their throats swollen, their eyes rolling like a newborn colt's, sweat running down their shoulders. Then they would fight. Spears flying, swords whonking, arrows raining from the windows and doors of the meadhall and the edge of the woods. Horses reared and fell over screaming, ravens flew, crazy as bats in a fire, men staggered, gesturing wildly, making speeches, dying or sometimes pretending to be dying, sneaking off. Sometimes the attackers would be driven back, sometimes they'd win and burn the meadhall down, sometimes they'd capture the king of the meadhall and make his people give weapons and gold rings and cows.

It was confusing and frightening, not in a way I could untangle. I was safe in my tree, and the men who fought were nothing to me, except of course that they talked in something akin to my language, which meant that we were, incredibly, related. I was sickened, if only at the waste of it: all they killed—cows, horses, men—they left to rot or burn. I sacked all I could and tried to store it, but my mother would growl and make faces because of the stink.

The fighting went on all that summer and began again the next and again the next. Sometimes when a meadhall burned, the survivors would go to another meadhall and, stretching out their hands, would crawl unarmed up the strangers' hill and would beg to be taken in. They would give the strangers whatever weapons or pigs or cattle they'd saved from destruction, and the strangers would give them an outbuilding, the worst of their food, and some straw. The two groups would fight as allies after that, except that now and then they betrayed each other, one shooting the other from behind for some reason, or stealing the other group's gold, some midnight, or sneaking into bed with the other group's wives and daughters.

I watched it, season after season. Sometimes I watched from the high cliff wall, where I could look out and see all the meadhall lights on the various hills across the countryside, glowing like candles, reflected stars. With luck, I might see, on a soft summer night, as many as three halls burning down at once. That was rare, of course. It grew rarer as the pattern of their warring changed. Hrothgar, who'd begun hardly stronger than the others, began to outstrip the rest. He'd worked out a theory about what fighting was for, and now he no longer fought with his six closest neighbors. He'd shown them the strength of his organization, and now, instead of making war on them, he sent men to them every three months or so, with heavy wagons and back-slings, to gather their tribute to his greatness. They piled his wagons high with gold and leather and weapons, and they kneeled to his messengers and made long speeches and promised to defend him against any foolhardy outlaw that dared to attack him. Hrothgar's messengers answered with friendly words and praise of the man they'd just plundered, as if the whole thing had been his idea, then whipped up the oxen, pulled up their loaded back-slings, and started home. It was a hard trip. The tall, silky grass of the meadows and the paths along the forest would clog the heavy wagon spokes and snarl the oxen's hooves; wagon wheels sunk in the rich black earth that only the wind had ever yet seeded or harvested. The oxen rolled their eyes, floundering, and mooed. Men swore. They pushed at the wheels with long oak poles and slashed at the oxen till their backs were crosshatched with bleeding welts and their noses ran pink foam. Sometimes with one terrific heave, an ox would break free of the traces and plunge into the brush. A man on a horse would go after it, slashed by branches, cutting through tangles of hazel and hawthorn, his horse balking at the pain of thorns, and sometimes when the man found the ox he would fill it with arrows and leave it to the wolves. Sometimes he merely sat, when he found the ox, and met its stupid, gloomy eyes and wept. Sometimes a horse, mired to the waist, would give up and merely stand, head hanging, as if waiting for death, and the men would howl at it and cut it with whips, or throw stones, or club it with heavy limbs, until finally one of them came to his senses and calmed the others, and they would winch out the horse with ropes and wagon wheels, if they could, or else abandon the horse or kill it—first stripping off the saddle and bridle and the handsomely decorated harness. At times, when a wagon was hopelessly mired, the men would walk back to Hrothgar's hall for help. When they returned, the wagon would be emptied of all its gold and burned, sometimes by people of Hrothgar's own tribe, though usually by others, and the oxen and horses would be dead.

Hrothgar met with his council for many nights and days, and they drank and talked and prayed to their curious carved-out creatures and finally came to a decision. They built roads. The kings from whom they'd taken tributes of treasure they now asked for tributes of men. Then Hrothgar and his neighbors, loaded like ants on a long march, pushed foot by foot and day by day around the marshes and over the moors and through the woods, pressing flat rocks into the soft ground and grass, and packing smaller stones around the rocks' sides, until, from my watch on the wall of the cliff, Hrothgar's whole realm was like a wobbly, lopsided wheel with spokes of stone.

And now when enemies from farther out struck at kings who called themselves Hrothgar's friends, a messenger would slip out and ride through the night to the tribute-taker, and in half an hour, while the enemy bands were still shouting at each other, still waving their ashspears, and saying what horrible things they would do, the forest would rumble with the sound of Hrothgar's horsemen. He would overcome them: his band had grown large, and for the treasures Hrothgar could afford now to give them in sign of his thanks, his warriors became hornets. New roads snaked out. New meadhalls gave tribute. His treasure-hoard grew till his meadhall was piled to the rafters with brightly painted shields and ornamented swords and boar's-head helmets and coils of gold, and they had to abandon the meadhall and sleep in the outbuildings. Meanwhile, those who paid tribute to him were forced to strike at more distant hills to gather the gold they paid to Hrothgar—and a little on the side for themselves. His power overran the world, from the foot of my cliff to the northern sea to the impenetrable forests south and east. They hacked down trees in widening rings around their central halls and blistered the land with peasant huts and pigpen fences till the forest looked like an old dog dying of mange. They thinned out the game, killed birds for sport, set accidental fires that would burn for days. Their sheep killed hedges, snipped valleys bare, and their pigs nosed up the very roots of what might have grown. Hrothgar's tribe made boats to drive farther north and west. There was nothing to stop the advance of man. Huge boars fled at the click of a harness. Wolves would cower in the glens like foxes when they caught that deadly scent. I was filled with a wordless, obscurely murderous unrest.

One night, inevitably, a blind man turned up at Hrothgar's temporary meadhall. He was carrying a harp. I watched from the shadow of a cowshed, since on that hill there were no trees. The guards at the door crossed their axes in front of him. He waited, smiling foolishly, while a messenger went inside. A few minutes later the messenger returned, gave the old man a grunt, and—cautiously, feeling ahead of himself with his crooked bare toes like a man engaged in some strange, pious dance, the foolish smile still fixed on his face—the blind old man went in. A boy darted up from the weeds at the foot of the hill, the harper's companion. He too was shown in.

The hall became quiet, and after a moment Hrothgar spoke, tones low and measured—of necessity, from too much shouting on midnight raids. The harper gave him back some answer, and Hrothgar spoke again. I glanced at the watchdogs. They still sat silent as treestumps, locked in my spell. I crept closer to the hall to hear. The people were noisy for a time, yelling to the harper, offering him mead, making jokes, and then again King Hrothgar spoke, white-bearded. The hall became still.

The silence expanded. People coughed. As if all by itself, then, the harp made a curious run of sounds, almost words, and then a moment later,

arresting as a voice from a hollow tree, the harper
began to chant:

Lo, we have heard the honor of the Speardanes,
nation-kings, in days now gone,
how those battle-lords brought themselves glory.
Oft Scyld Shefing shattered the forces
of kinsman-marauders, dragged away their
meadhall-benches, terrified earls—after first men found
him castaway. (He got recompense for that!)
He grew up under the clouds, won glory of men
till all his enemies sitting around him
heard across the whaleroads his demands and gave
him tribute. That was a good king!

So he sang—or intoned, with the harp behind
him—twisting together like sailors' ropes the
bits and pieces of the best old songs. The people
were hushed. Even the surrounding hills were
hushed, as if brought low by language. He knew
his art. He was king of the Shapers, harpstring
scratchers (oakmoss-bearded, inspired by winds).
That was what had brought him over wilderness,
down blindman's alleys of time and space, to
Hrothgar's famous hall. He would sing the glory
of Hrothgar's line and gild his wisdom and stir
up his men to more daring deeds, for a price.

He told how Scyld by the cunning of arms
had rebuilt the old Danish kingdom from ashes,
lordless a long time before he came, and the prey
of every passing band, and how Scyld's son by
the strength of his wits had increased their power,
a man who fully understood men's need, from
lust to love, and knew how to use it to fashion a
mile-wide fist of chain-locked steel. He sang of
battles and marriages, of funerals and hangings,

the whimperings of beaten enemies, of splendid hunts and harvests. He sang of Hrothgar, hoarfrost white, magnificent of mind.

When he finished, the hall was quiet as a mound. I too was silent, my ear pressed tight against the timbers. Even to me, incredibly, he had made it all seem true and very fine. Now a little, now more, a great roar began, an exhalation of breath that swelled to a rumble of voices and then to the howling and clapping and stomping of men gone mad on art. They would seize the oceans, the farthest stars, the deepest secret rivers in Hrothgar's name! Men wept like children: children sat stunned. It went on and on, a fire more dread than any visible fire.

Only one man in the kingdom seemed cast down: the man who'd been Hrothgar's harper before the blind man came to make his bid. The former harper crept out into the darkness, unnoticed by the rest. He slipped away through fields and forests, his precious old instrument under his arm, to seek out refuge in the hall of some lesser marauder. I too crept away, my mind aswim in ringing phrases, magnificent, golden, and all of them, incredibly, lies.

What was he? The man had changed the world, had torn up the past by its thick, gnarled roots and had transmuted it, and they, who knew the truth, remembered it his way—and so did I.

I crossed the moors in a queer panic, like a creature half insane. I knew the truth. *It was late spring. Every sheep and goat had its wobbly twins. A man said, "I'll steal their gold and burn their meadhall!" and another man said, "Do it now!"* I remember the ragged men fighting each other till the snow was red slush, whining in winter, the shriek of people and animals burning, the whip-slashed oxen in the mire, the scattered battle-leavings: wolf-torn corpses, falcons fat with blood. Yet I also remembered, as if it had happened, great Scyld, of whose kingdom no trace remained, and his farsighted son, of whose greater kingdom no trace remained. And the stars overhead were alive with the promise of Hrothgar's vast power, his universal peace. The moors their axes had stripped of trees glowed silver in the moonlight, and the yellow lights of peasant huts were like scattered jewels on the ravendark cloak of a king. I was so filled with sorrow and tenderness I could hardly have found it in my heart to snatch a pig!

Thus I fled, ridiculous hairy creature torn apart by poetry—crawling, whimpering, streaming tears, across the world like a two-headed beast, like mixed-up lamb and kid at the tail of a baffled, indifferent ewe—and I gnashed my teeth and clutched the sides of my head as if to heal the split, but I couldn't.

There was a Scyld, once, who ruled the Danes; and other men ruled after him, that much was true. And the rest?

At the top of the cliffwall I turned and looked down, and I saw all the lights of Hrothgar's realm and the realms beyond that, that would soon be his, and to clear my mind, I sucked in wind and screamed. The sound went out, violent, to the rims of the world, and after a moment it bounced back up at me—harsh and ungodly against the sigh of the remembered harp—like a thousand tortured rat-squeals crying: *Lost!*

I clamped my palms to my ears and stretched
up my lips and shrieked again: a stab at truth,
a snatch at apocalyptic glee. Then I ran on all
fours, chest pounding, to the smoky mere.

4

He sings to a heavier harpsong now, old heart-
string scratcher, memory scraper. Of the richest
of kings made sick of soul by the scattered bones
of thanes. By late afternoon the fire dies down
and the column of smoke is white, no longer
greasy. There will be others this year, they know;
yet they hang on. The sun backs away from the
world like a crab and the days grow shorter, the
nights grow longer, more dark and dangerous. I
smile, angry in the thickening dusk, and feast
my eyes on the greatest of meadhalls, unsatisfied.

His pride. The torch of kingdoms. Hart.

The Shaper remains, though now there are nobler
courts where he might sing. The pride of creation.
He built this hall by the power of his songs:
created with casual words its grave mor(t)ality.
The boy observes him, tall and solemn, twelve
years older than the night he first crept in with
his stone-eyed master. He knows no art but tragedy—a moving singer. The credit is wholly mine.

Inspired by winds (or whatever you please), the
old man sang of a glorious meadhall whose light

would shine to the ends of the ragged world. The thought took seed in Hrothgar's mind. It grew. He called all his people together and told them his daring scheme. He would build a magnificent meadhall high on a hill, with a view of the western sea, a victory-seat near the giants' work, old ruined fortress from the world's first war, to stand forever as a sign of glory and justice of Hrothgar's Danes. There he would sit and give treasures out, all wealth but the lives of men and the people's land. And so his sons would do after him, and his sons' sons, to the final generation.

I listened, huddled in the darkness, tormented, mistrustful. I knew them, had watched them; yet the things he said seemed true. He sent to far kingdoms for woodsmen, carpenters, metalsmiths, goldsmiths—also carters, victualers, clothiers to attend to the workmen—and for weeks their uproar filled the days and nights. I watched from the vines and boulders of the giants' ruin, two miles off. Then word went out to the races of men that Hrothgar's hall was finished. He gave it its name. From neighboring realms and from across the sea came men to the great celebration. The harper sang.

I listened, felt myself swept up. I knew very well that all he said was ridiculous, not light for their darkness but flattery, illusion, a vortex pulling them from sunlight to heat, a kind of midsummer burgeoning, waltz to the sickle. Yet I was swept up. "Ridiculous!" I hissed in the black of the forest. I snatched up a snake from beside my foot and whispered to it, "I knew him *when!*" But I couldn't bring out a wicked cackle, as I'd meant to do. My heart was light with Hrothgar's goodness, and leaden with grief at my own bloodthirsty ways. I backed away, crablike, further into darkness—like a crab retreating in pain when you strike two stones at the mouth of his underwater den. I backed away till the honeysweet lure of the harp no longer mocked me. Yet even now my mind was tormented by images. Thanes filled the hall and a great silent crowd of them spilled out over the surrounding hill, smiling, peaceable, hearing the harper as if not a man in all that lot had ever twisted a knife in his neighbor's chest.

"Well then he's changed them," I said, and stumbled and fell on the root of a tree. "Why not?"

Why not? the forest whispered back—yet not the forest, something deeper, an impression from another mind, some live thing old and terrible.

I listened, tensed.

Not a sound.

"He reshapes the world," I whispered, belligerent. "So his name implies. He stares strange-eyed at the mindless world and turns dry sticks to gold."

A little poetic, I would readily admit. His manner of speaking was infecting me, making me pompous. "Nevertheless," I whispered crossly—but I couldn't go on, too conscious all at once of my whispering, my eternal posturing, always transforming the world with words—changing nothing. I still had the snake in my fist. I set it down. It fled.

"He takes what he finds," I said stubbornly, trying again. "And by changing men's minds he makes the best of it. Why not?" But it sounded petulant; and it wasn't true, I knew. He sang for

pay, for the praise of women—one in particular—
and for the honor of a famous king's hand on his
arm. If the ideas of art were beautiful, that was
art's fault, not the Shaper's. A blind selector,
almost mindless: a bird. Did they murder each
other more gently because in the woods sweet
songbirds sang?

Yet I wasn't satisfied. His fingers picked in-
fallibly, as if moved by something beyond his
power, and the words stitched together out of
ancient songs, the scenes interwoven out of dreary
tales, made a vision without seams, an image of
himself yet not-himself, beyond the need of any
shaggy old gold-friend's pay: the projected possible.

"Why not?" I whispered, jerking forward, struggling to make my eyes sear through the dark
trunks and vines.

I could feel it all around me, that invisible presence, chilly as the first intimation of death, the
dusty unblinking eyes of a thousand snakes.
There was no sound. I touched a fat, slick loop
of vine, prepared to leap back in horror, but it
was only vine, no worse. And still no sound, no
movement. I got up on my feet, bent over,
squinting, and edged back through the trees toward the town. It followed me—whatever it was.
I was as sure of that as I'd ever been of anything.
And then, in one instant, as if it had all been my
mind, the thing was gone. In the hall they were
laughing.

Men and women stood talking in the light of
the meadhall door and on the narrow streets
below; on the lower hillside boys and girls played
near the sheep pens, shyly holding hands. A few
lay touching each other in the forest eaves. I

thought how they'd shriek if I suddenly showed
my face, and it made me smile, but I held myself
back. They talked nothing, stupidities, their soft
voices groping like hands. I felt myself tightening,
cross, growing restless for no clear reason, and I
made myself move more slowly. Then, circling
the clearing, I stepped on something fleshy, and
jerked away. It was a man. They'd cut his throat.
His clothes had been stolen. I stared up at the
hall, baffled, beginning to shake. They went on
talking softly, touching hands, their hair full of
light. I lifted up the body and slung it across
my shoulder.

Then the harp began to play. The crowd grew
still.

The harp sighed, the old man sang, as sweet-
voiced as a child.

He told of how the earth was first built, long
ago: said that the greatest of gods made the world,
every wonder-bright plain and the turning seas, and
set out as signs of his victory the sun and moon,
great lamps for light to land-dwellers, kingdom
torches, and adorned the fields with all colors and
shapes, made limbs and leaves and gave life to
the every creature that moves on land.

The harp turned solemn. He told of an ancient
feud between two brothers which split all the
world between darkness and light. And I, Grendel,
was the dark side, he said in effect. The terrible
race God cursed.

I believed him. Such was the power of the
Shaper's harp! I stood wriggling my face, letting
tears down my nose, grinding my fists into my
streaming eyes, even though to do it I had to
squeeze with my elbow the corpse of the proof
that both of us were cursed, or neither, that the

brothers had never lived, nor the god who judged them. "Waaa!" I bawled.

Oh what a conversion!

I staggered out into the open and up toward the hall with my burden, groaning out, "Mercy! Peace!" The harper broke off, the people screamed. (They have their own versions, but this is the truth.) Drunken men rushed me with battle-axes. I sank to my knees, crying, "Friend! Friend!" They hacked at me, yipping like dogs. I held up the body for protection. Their spears came through it and one of them nicked me, a tiny scratch high on my left breast, but I knew by the sting it had venom on it and I understood, as shocked as I'd been the first time, that they could kill me—eventually *would* if I gave them a chance. I struck at them, holding the body as a shield, and two fell bleeding from my nails at the first little swipe. The others backed off. I crushed the body in my hug, then hurled it in their faces, turned, and fled. They didn't follow.

I ran to the center of the forest and fell down panting. My mind was wild. "Pity," I moaned, "O pity! pity!" I wept—strong monster with teeth like a shark's—and I slammed the earth with such force that a seam split open twelve feet long. "Bastards!" I roared. "Sons of bitches! Fuckers!" Words I'd picked up from men in their rages. I wasn't even sure what they meant, though I had an idea: defiance, rejection of the gods that, for my part, I'd known all along to be lifeless sticks. I roared with laughter, still sobbing. We, the accursed, didn't even have words for swearing in! "*AAARGH!*" I whooped, then covered my ears and hushed. It sounded silly.

My sudden awareness of my foolishness made me calm.

I looked up through the treetops, ludicrously hopeful. I think I was half prepared, in my dark, demented state, to see God, bearded and gray as geometry, scowling down at me, shaking his bloodless finger.

"Why can't I have someone to talk to?" I said. The stars said nothing, but I pretended to ignore the rudeness. "The Shaper has people to talk to," I said. I wrung my fingers. "Hrothgar has people to talk to."

I thought about it.

Perhaps it wasn't true.

As a matter of fact, if the Shaper's vision of goodness and peace was a part of himself, not idle rhymes, then no one understood him at all, not even Hrothgar. And as for Hrothgar, if he was serious about his idea of glory—sons and sons' sons giving out treasure—I had news for him. If he had sons, they wouldn't hear his words. They would weigh his silver and gold in their minds. I've watched the generations. I've seen their weasel eyes.

I fought down my smile.

"That could change," I said, shaking my finger as if at an audience. "The Shaper may yet improve men's minds, bring peace to the miserable Danes."

But they were doomed, I knew, and I was glad. No denying it. Let them wander the fogroads of Hell.

* * *

Two nights later I went back. I was addicted. The

Shaper was singing the glorious deeds of the dead men, praising war. He sang how they'd fought me. It was all lies. The sly harp rasped like snakes in cattails, glorifying death. I snatched a guard and smashed him on a tree, but my stomach turned at the thought of eating him. "Woe to the man," the Shaper sang, "who shall through wicked hostilities shove his soul down into the fire's hug! Let him hope for no change: he can never turn away! But lucky the man who, after his deathday, shall seek the Prince, find peace in his father's embrace!"

"Bullshit!" I whispered through clenched teeth. How was it that he could enrage me so?

Why not? the darkness hissed around me. *Why not? Why not?* Teasing, tormenting, as cold as a dead hand closing on my wrist.

Imagination, I knew. Some evil inside myself pushed out into the trees. I knew what I knew, the mindless, mechanical bruteness of things, and when the harper's lure drew my mind away to hopeful dreams, the dark of what was and always was reached out and snatched my feet.

And yet I'd be surprised, I had to admit, if anything in myself could be as cold, as dark, as centuries old as the presence I felt around me. I touched a vine to reassure myself. It was a snake. I snapped back in terror.

Then I calmed myself again. The fangs hadn't hit. It came to me that the presence was still there, somewhere deeper, much deeper, in the night. I had a feeling that if I let myself I could fall toward it, that it was pulling me, pulling the whole world in like a whirlpool.

Craziness, of course. I got up, though the feeling was as strong as ever, and felt my way back through the forest and over to the cliffwall and back to the mere and to my cave. I lay there listening to the indistinct memory of the Shaper's songs. My mother picked through the bone pile, sullen. I'd brought no food.

"Ridiculous," I whispered.

She looked at me.

It was a cold-blooded lie that a god had lovingly made the world and set out the sun and moon as lights to land-dwellers, that brothers had fought, that one of the races was saved, the other cursed. Yet he, the old Shaper, might make it true, by the sweetness of his harp, his cunning trickery. It came to me with a fierce jolt that I wanted it. As they did too, though vicious animals, cunning, cracked with theories. I wanted it, yes! Even if I must be the outcast, cursed by the rules of his hideous fable.

She whimpered, scratched at the nipple I had not sucked in years. She was pitiful, foul, her smile a jagged white tear in the firelight: waste.

She whimpered one sound: *Dool-dool! Dool-dool!*, scratching at her bosom, a ghastly attempt to climb back up to speech.

I clamped my eyes shut, listened to the river, and after a time I slept.

I sat up with a jerk.

The thing was all around me, now, like a thunder charge.

"Who is it?" I said.

No answer. Darkness.

My mother was asleep; she was as deadlooking as a red-gray old sea-elephant stretched on the shore of a summer day.

I got up and silently left the cave. I went to the cliffwall, then down to the moor.

Still nothing.

I made my mind a blank and fell, sank away like a stone through earth and sea, toward the dragon.

5

No use of a growl, a whoop, a roar, in the presence of that beast! Vast, red-golden, huge tail coiled, limbs sprawled over his treasure-hoard, eyes not firey but cold as the memory of family deaths. Vanishing away across invisible floors, there were things of gold, gems, jewels, silver vessels the color of blood in the undulant, dragon-red light. Arching above him the ceiling and upper walls of his cave were alive with bats. The color of his sharp scales darkened and brightened as the dragon inhaled and exhaled slowly, drawing new air across his vast internal furnace; his razor-sharp tusks gleamed and glinted as if they too, like the mountains beneath him, were formed of precious stones and metals.

My heart shook. His eyes stared straight at me. My knees and insides were so weak I had to drop down on all fours. His mouth opened slightly. Bits of flame escaped.

"Ah, Grendel!" he said. "You've come." The voice was startling. No rolling boom, as I would have expected, but a voice that might have come from an old, old man. Louder, of course, but not much louder.

"We've been expecting you," he said. He gave a nervous laugh, like a miser caught at his counting. His eyes were heavy-lidded, minutely veined, wrinkled like an elderly mead-drinker's. "Stand around the side, if you don't mind, boy," he said. "I get a cough sometimes, and it's terrible straight out front." The high dead eyelids wrinkled more, the corners of his mouth snaked up as he chuckled, sly, hardly hiding his malice. I quickly ducked around to the side.

"Good boy," he said. He tipped his head, lowering an eye toward me. "*Smart* boy! He he he!" He lifted a wrinkled paw with man-length talons for nails and held it over my head as if to crush me with it, but he merely brought it down lightly, once, twice, three times, patting my head.

"Well, speak, boy," he said. "Say 'Hello there, Mr. Dragon!'" He cackled.

My throat convulsed and I tried to get my breath to speak, but I couldn't.

The dragon smiled. Horrible, debauched, mouth limp and cracked, loose against the teeth as an ancient dog's. "Now you know how *they* feel when they see *you*, eh? Scared enough to pee in their pants! He he!" He looked startled by an unpleasant thought, then cross. "You didn't, did you?"

I shook my head.

"Good," he said. "That's valuable stuff you're standing on. Boobies, hemorrhoids, boils, slaver (nyeh heh heh) . . . *Now*." He moved his head as if adjusting his flaking neck to a tight metal collar and put on what looked like, for him, a sober expression, like an old drunk preparing a solemn

face for court. Then, as if involuntarily, he cackled
again. It was horrible, horrible! Obscene! He
couldn't stop himself. He cackled so hard a bril-
liant tear like a giant diamond rolled down his
cheek. And still he couldn't stop. He raised up the
taloned paw and pointed at me. His head tipped
back, laughing, blowing fire out his mouth and
nostrils. He tried to say something, but the laughing got worse. He rolled over on his side, stretching
up one vast, wrinkled wing for balance, covering
his eyes with one claw, still pointing with the
other, roaring with laughter and kicking a little
with his two back feet. I felt cross all at once,
though I didn't dare show it. "Like a rabbit!" he
brought out. "Nyee he he he! When you're scared,
you look—nyee he he he—exactly . . . (*gasp!*)
exactly . . ."

I scowled and, realizing I had my hands out in
front of me like a rabbit sitting up, I jerked
them behind my back. My scowl of rage nearly
finished him. He hooted, gasped, sobbed, began to
choke with laughter. I forgot myself completely.
I snatched up an emerald the size of a fist and
pulled it back to throw it at him. He was sober
instantly. "Put it down!" he said. He drew in
breath and turned his huge head straight at me. I
dropped it and fought to keep my bowels from
moving down.

"Don't touch," he said. The old-man voice was
as terrible now as the eyes. It was as if he'd
been dead for a thousand years. "Never never
never touch my things," he said. Flame came out
with the words and singed the hair on my belly
and legs. I nodded, trembling all over. "Good," he
said. He stared at me a moment longer, then slowly,

slowly turned his head away. Then, old womanish, as if he were, though still spiteful, slightly embarrassed, he got back up onto his treasure pile, stretched out his wings, and settled.

He was in the foulest of moods. I doubted that I could learn anything from him now. I'd be lucky to get away alive. I thought all at once about what he'd said: "Now you know how *they* feel when they see *you*." He had a point. From now on I'd stay clear of them. It was one thing to eat one from time to time—that was only natural: kept them from overpopulating, maybe starving to death, come winter—but it was another thing to scare them, give them heart attacks, fill their nights with nightmares, just for sport.

"Fiddlesticks," the dragon said.

I blinked.

"Fiddlesticks, that's what I said," he repeated. "Why *not* frighten them? Creature, I could tell you things . . ." He rolled his eyes up under the heavy lids and made a noise. "*Glaagh.*" He remained that way, breathing hard with peevish anger. "Stupid, stupid, *stupid!*" he hissed. "The whole damned kit and caboodle. Why did you come here? Why do you bother me?—Don't answer!" he added quickly, stopping me. "I know what's in your mind. I know everything. That's what makes me so sick and old and tired."

"I'm sorry," I said.

"Be still!" he screamed. Flame shot clear to the cavemouth. "I know you're sorry. For right now, that is. For this one frail, foolish flicker-flash in the long dull fall of eternity. I'm unimpressed—No no! Be still!" His eye burst open like a hole, to hush me. I closed my mouth. The eye was terrible, lowering toward me. I felt as if I were tumbling down into it—dropping endlessly down through a soundless void. He let me fall, down and down toward a black sun and spiders, though he knew I was beginning to die. Nothing could have been more disinterested: serpent to the core.

But then he spoke after all, or rather laughed, and reality snapped back. Laughed, spoke, and broke my fall not as a kindness to me but because of his cold pleasure in knowing what he knew. I was in the cave again, and his horrible smile was snaking up his wrinkled cheek and his eye was once more half-closed. "You want the word," he said. "That's what you've come for. My advice is, don't ask! Do as I do! Seek out gold—but not *my* gold—and guard it!"

"Why?" I said.

"BE STILL!" The cave went white with his fire, and the rock walls roared the echo back. Bats flew like dust in a granary, then returned to their places, a few at a time, until all was still again, motionless, as if lifeless. His wings, which had stretched out slightly, relaxed and settled.

I waited for what seemed hours, huddling, my fingers protecting my head.

Then: "You want to know about the Shaper."

I nodded.

"Illusion," he said. He half smiled, then let it go as if infinitely weary, sick of Time. "I know everything, you see," the old voice wheedled. "The beginning, the present, the end. Everything. You now, you see the past and the present, like other low creatures: no higher faculties than memory and perception. But dragons, my boy, have a whole different kind of mind." He stretched his mouth in a kind of smile, no trace of pleasure in it. "We see from the mountaintop: all time, all space. We see in one instant the passionate vision and the blowout. Not that we *cause* things to fail, you understand." He was testy all at once, as if answering an argument that had been put to him so often he was sick of it. "Dragons don't mess with your piddling free will. Pah! Listen to me, boy." The dead eye brightened. "If you with your knowledge of present and past recall that a certain man slipped on, say, a banana peel, or fell off his chair, or drowned in a river, that recollection does not mean that you *caused* him to slip, or fall, or drown. Correct? Of course it's correct! It happened, and you know it, but knowledge is not *cause*. Of course! Anyone who argues otherwise is a stupid ignoramus. Well, so with me. My knowledge of the future does not *cause* the future. It merely *sees* it, exactly as creatures at your low level recall things past. And even if, say, I interfere—burn up somebody's mead-hall, for instance, whether because I just feel like it or because some supplicant asked me to— even then I do not change the future, I merely do what I saw from the beginning. That's obvious, surely. Let's say it's settled then. So much for free will and intercession!"

The dragon's eye closed to a slit. "Grendel!"

I jumped.

"Don't look so bored," he said. He scowled, black as midnight. "Think how *I* must feel," he said.

I almost said "I'm sorry," but caught myself.

"Man," he said, then left a long pause, letting scorn build up in the cave like the venom in his breath. "I can see you understand them. Counters, measurers, theory-makers.

All pigs eat cheese.
Old Snaggle is a pig.
If Snaggle is sick and refuses to eat, try cheese.

Games, games, games!" He snorted fire. "They only think they think. No total vision, total system, merely schemes with a vague family resemblance, no more identity than bridges and, say, spider-webs. But they rush across chasms on spiderwebs, and sometimes they make it, and that, they think, settles that! I could tell you a thousand tiresome stories of their absurdity. They'd map out roads through Hell with their crackpot theories, their here-to-the-moon-and-back lists of paltry facts. Insanity—the simplest insanity ever devised! Simple facts in isolation, and facts to connect them—ands and buts—are the *sine qua non* of all their glorious achievement. But there are no such facts. Con-nectedness is the essence of everything. It doesn't stop them, of course. They build the whole world out of teeth deprived of bodies to chew or be chewed on.

"They sense that, of course, from time to time; have uneasy feelings that all they live by is non-sense. They have dim apprehensions that such proprositions as 'God does not exist' are somewhat dubious at least in comparison with statements like 'All carnivorous cows eat meat.' That's where the Shaper saves them. Provides an illusion of re-ality—puts together all their facts with a gluey whine of connectedness. Mere tripe, believe me. Mere sleight-of-wits. He knows no more than they do about total reality—less, if anything: works with the same old clutter of atoms, the givens of his time and place and tongue. But he spins it all together with harp runs and hoots, and they think what they think is alive, think Heaven loves them. It keeps them going—for what that's worth. As for myself, I can hardly bear to look."

"I see," I said. It was to some extent untrue.

The dragon smiled, seemed almost friendly for an instant. "You've been very attentive and thoughtful," he said, "all things considered. So I will tell you about Time and Space."

"Thank you," I said, as heartily as I could manage. I had more than enough to think about, it seemed to me.

He scowled, and I said no more. He took a deep breath, shifted his forelegs to a position more comfortable, and, after a moment's thought, began:

"In all discussions of Nature, we must try to remember the differences of scale, and in particular the differences of time-span. We (by which I mean you, not us) are apt to take modes of observable functioning in our own bodies as setting an absolute scale. But as a matter of fact, it's extremely rash to extend conclusions derived from observation far beyond the scale of magnitude to which the observation was confined. For example, the apparent absence of change within a second of time tells nothing as to the change within a thousand years. Also, no appearance of change within a thousand years tells anything concerning what might happen in, say, a million years; and no apparent change within a million years tells anything about a million million years. We can extend this progression indefinitely; there is no absolute standard of magnitude. Any term in this progression is large compared to its predecessor and small compared to its successor.

"Again, all special studies presuppose certain fundamental types of things. (Here I am using the word 'thing,' notice, in its most general sense, which can include activities, colors, and all other senses, also values.) As lower minds function, study, or 'science,' is concerned with a limited set of various types of things. There is thus, in the first place, this variety of types. In the second place, there is the determination as to what types are exhibited in any indicated situation. For example, there is the singular proposition—'This is green'—and there is the more general proposition—'All those things are green.' This type of inquiry is what your usual reasoning takes care of. Undoubtedly such inquiries are essential in the initial stage of any study, for lower minds. But every such study must strive to get beyond it. Unfortunately—"

He glanced at me, suspicious. "You're not paying attention."

"I am!" I said, clasping my hands to show my seriousness.

But he shook his head slowly. "Nothing interests you but excitement, violence."

"That's not true!" I said.

His eye opened wider, his body brightened from end to end. "*You* tell *me* what's true?" he said.

"I'm trying to follow. I do my best," I said. "You should be reasonable. What do you expect?"

The dragon thought about it, breathing slowly, full of wrath. At last he closed his eyes. "Let us try starting somewhere else," he said. "It's damned hard, you understand, confining myself to

concepts familiar to a creature of the Dark Ages.
Not that one age is darker than another. Technical jargon from another dark age." He scowled as
if hardly capable of forcing himself on. Then,
after a long moment: "The essence of life is to
be found in the frustrations of established order.
The universe refuses the deadening influence of
complete conformity. And yet in its refusal, it
passes toward novel order as a primary requisite
for important experience. We have to explain the
aim at forms of order, and the aim at novelty of
order, and the measure of success, and the measure of failure. Apart from some understanding,
however dim-witted, of these characteristics of
historic process . . ." His voice trailed off.

After another long pause, he said: "Approach
it this way. Let us take this jug." He picked up
a golden vessel and held it toward me, not letting
me touch it. In spite of himself, as it seemed, he
looked hostile and suspicious, as if he thought I
might perhaps be so stupid as to snatch the thing
and run. "How does this jug differ from something animate?" He drew it back out of reach.
"By organization! Exactly! This jug is an absolute
democracy of atoms. It has importance, or thereness, so to speak, but no Expression, or, loosely,
ah-ha!-ness. Importance is primarily monistic in its
reference to the universe. Limited to a finite individual occasion, importance ceases to be important. In some sense or other—we can skip the
details—importance is derived from the immanence
of infinitude in the finite. Expression, however—
listen closely now—expression is founded on the
finite occasion. It is the activity of finitude impressing itself on its environment. Importance

passes from the world as one to the world as many, whereas expression is the gift from the world as many to the world as one. The laws of nature are large average effects which reign impersonally. But there is nothing average about expression: it is essentially individual. Consider one definite molecule—"

"A what?" I said.

The closed eyes squeezed tight. He let out a long, cross sigh of red-orange fire.

"Put it this way," he said. His voice had grown feeble, as if he were losing hope. "In the case of vegetables, we find expressive bodily organizations which lack any one center of experience with a higher complexity either of expressions received or of inborn data. Another democracy, but with qualifications, as we shall see. An animal, on the other hand, is dominated by one or more centers of experience. If the dominant activity be severed from the rest of the body—if, for example, we cut off the head—the whole coordination collapses, and the animal dies. Whereas in the case of the vegetable, the democracy can be subdivided into minor democracies which easily survive without much apparent loss of functional expression." He paused. "You at *least* follow that?"

"I think so."

He sighed. "Listen. Listen closely! An angry man does not usually shake his fist at the universe in general. He makes a selection and knocks his neighbor down. A piece of rock, on the other hand, impartially attracts the universe according to the law of gravitation. You grant there's a difference?"

He waited, furious with impatience. I met his

eye as long as I could, then shook my head. It was unfair. For all I knew he might be telling me gibberish on purpose. I sat down. Let him babble. Let him burn me alive. The hell with it.

After a long, long time, he said, "It was stupid of you to come."

I nodded, sulking.

He stretched his wings—it was like a huge, irascible yawn—then settled again. "Things come and go," he said. "That's the gist of it. In a billion billion billion years, everything will have come and gone several times, in various forms. Even I will be gone. A certain man will absurdly kill me. A terrible pity—loss of a remarkable form of life. Conservationists will howl." He chuckled. "Meaningless, however. These jugs and pebbles, everything, these too will go. Poof! Boobies, hemorrhoids, boils, slaver . . ."

"You don't know that!" I said.

He smiled, showing all his teeth, and I knew he knew it.

"A swirl in the stream of time. A temporary gathering of bits, a few random dust specks, so to speak—pure metaphor, you understand—then by chance a vast floating cloud of dustspecks, an expanding universe—" He shrugged. "Complexities: green dust as well as the regular kind. Purple dust. Gold. Additional refinements: sensitive dust, copulating dust, *worshipful dust!*" He laughed, hollow as the cavern around him. "New laws for each new form, of course. New lines of potential. Complexity beyond complexity, accident on accident, until—" His leer was like icy wind.

"Go on," I said.

He closed his eyes, still smiling. "Pick an apocalypse, any apocalypse. A sea of black oil and dead things. No wind. No light. Nothing stirring, not even an ant, a spider. A silent universe. Such is the end of the flicker of time, the brief, hot fuse of events and ideas set off, accidentally, and snuffed out, accidentally, by man. Not a real ending of course, nor even a beginning. Mere ripple in Time's stream."

I squinted. "That really could happen?"

"It has happened," he said—and smiled as if it pleased him—"in the future. I am the witness."

I thought about it for a while, remembering the harp, then shook my head. "I don't believe you."

"It will come."

I went on squinting at him, hand on my mouth. He could lie. He was evil enough.

He shook his ponderous head. "Ah, man's cunning mind!" he said, and cackled. "Merely a new complexity, a new event, new set of nonce-rules generating further nonce-rules, down and down and down. Things lock on, you know. The Devonian fish, the juxtaposed thumb, the fontanel, technology—*click click, click click . . .*"

"I think you're lying," I said, confused again, aswirl in words.

"I noticed that. You'll never know. It must be very frustrating to be caged like a Chinaman's cricket in a limited mind." His cackle lacked spirit, this time. He was growing very weary of my presence.

"You said 'Fiddlesticks,'" I said. "Why is it fiddlesticks if I stop giving people heart attacks over nothing? Why shouldn't one change one's ways, improve one's character?" I must have been an interesting sight, that instant, big shaggy monster intense and earnest, bent like a priest at his prayers.

He shrugged. "Whatever you like. Do as you think best."

"But why?"

" 'Why? Why?' Ridiculous question! Why anything? My advice to you—"

I clenched my fists, though it was absurd, of course. One does not swing at dragons. *"No, why?"*

The dragon tipped up his great tusked head, stretched his neck, sighed fire. "Ah, Grendel!" he said. He seemed that instant almost to rise to pity. "You improve them, my boy! Can't you see that yourself? You stimulate them! You make them think and scheme. You drive them to poetry, science, religion, all that makes them what they are for as long as they last. You are, so to speak, the brute existent by which they learn to define themselves. The exile, captivity, death they shrink from—the blunt facts of their mortality, their abondonment—that's what you make them recognize, embrace! You *are* mankind, or man's condition: inseparable as the mountain-climber and the mountain. If you withdraw, you'll instantly be replaced. Brute existents, you know, are a dime a dozen. No sentimental trash, then. If man's the irrelevance that interests you, stick with him! Scare him to glory! It's all the same in the end, matter and motion, simple or complex. No difference, finally. Death, transfiguration. Ashes to ashes and slime to slime, amen."

I was sure he was lying. Or anyway half-sure. Flattering me into tormenting them because he, in his sullen hole, loved viciousness. I said, "Let them find some other 'brute existent,' whatever that is. I refuse."

"Do!" he said leering scornfully. "Do something else, by all means! Alter the future! Make the world a better place in which to live! Help the poor! Feed the hungry. Be kind to idiots! What a challenge!"

He no longer looked at me, no longer made any pretense of telling the truth. "Personally," he said, "my great ambition is to count all this"—he waved vaguely at the treasure around him—"and possibly sort it into piles. 'Know thyself,' that's my dictum. Know how much you've got, and beware of strangers!"

I scraped away rubies and emeralds with the side of my foot. "Let me tell you what the Shaper said."

"Spare me, I beg you!" He covered his ears with his claws, gave a hideous grin.

But I was stubborn. "He said that the greatest of gods made the world, every wonder-bright plain and the turning seas. He said—"

"Ridiculous."

"Why?"

"What god? Where? Life-force, you mean? The principle of process? God as the history of Chance?"

In some way that I couldn't explain, I knew that his scorn of my childish credulity was right.

"Nevertheless, something will come of all this," I said.

"Nothing," he said. "A brief pulsation in the black hole of eternity. My advice to you—"

"Wait and see," I said.

He shook his head. "My advice to you, my violent friend, is to seek out gold and sit on it."

6

Nothing was changed, everything was changed, by my having seen the dragon. It's one thing to listen, full of scorn and doubt, to poets' versions of time past and visions of time to come; it's another to know, as coldly and simply as my mother knows her pile of bones, what is. Whatever I may have understood or misunderstood in the dragon's talk, something much deeper stayed with me, became my aura. Futility, doom, became a smell in the air, pervasive and acrid as the dead smell after a forest fire—my scent and the world's, the scent of trees, rocks, waterways wherever I went.

But there was one thing worse. I discovered that the dragon had put a charm on me: no weapon could cut me. I could walk up to the meadhall whenever I pleased, and they were powerless. My heart became darker because of that. Though I scorned them, sometimes hated them, there had been something between myself and men when we could fight. Now, invulnerable, I was as solitary as one live tree in a vast landscape of coal.

Needless to say, I misunderstood in the beginning: I thought it an advantage.

It was the height of summer, harvest season in the first year of what I have come to call my war with Hrothgar. The night air was filled with the smell of apples and shocked grain, and I could hear the noise in the meadhall from a mile away. I moved toward it, drawn as always, as if by some kind of curse. I meant not to be seen that night. For all the dragon's talk, I had no intention of terrifying Hrothgar's thanes for nothing. (I had not begun, at that time, my systematic raids. In fact I hadn't yet admitted to myself that it was war. I killed stragglers now and then—with a certain grim pleasure very different from that which I got from cracking a cow's skull—but I'd never yet struck at the hall, hadn't even revealed myself there—except on that one ridiculous night when I walked up and tried to join them.) I hunkered down at the edge of the forest, looking up the long hill at the meadhall lights. I could hear the Shaper's song.

I no longer remember exactly what he sang. I know only that it had a strange effect on me: it no longer filled me with doubt and distress, loneliness, shame. It enraged me. It was their confidence, maybe—their blissful, swinish ignorance, their bumptious, self-satisfaction, and, worst of all, their *hope*. I went closer, darting from cowshed to cowshed and finally up to the wall. I found a crack and peeked in. I do remember what he said, now that I think about it. Or some of it. He spoke of how God had been kind to the Scyldings, sending so rich a harvest. The people sat beaming, bleary-eyed and fat, nodding their approval of God. He spoke of God's great generosity in sending them so wise a king. They all raised their cups to God and Hrothgar, and Hrothgar smiled, bits of food in his beard. The Shaper talked of how God had vanquished their enemies and filled up their houses with precious treasure, how they were the richest, most powerful people on earth, how here and here alone in all the world men were free and heroes were brave and virgins were virgins. He ended the song, and people clapped and shouted their praise and filled their golden cups. All around their bubble of stupidity I could feel the brume of the dragon.

Then a stick snapped behind me, and the same instant, a dog barked. A helmeted, chain-mailed guard leaped out at me, sword in two hands above his head, prepared to split me. I jerked back, but there was something in the way, and I fell. I tried to roll, and then, out of the corner of my eye, I saw the sword coming and I knew I couldn't escape it. I went limp, the way animals sometimes do at the moment of the predator's leap. Nothing happened.

I was as surprised as the guard. We both stared, I sprawling helpless on my back, the sword across my belly, the guard leaning forward, still holding the hilt as if afraid to let it go. His beard and nose stuck out through the cheekplates, and his eyes, in the shadowed recess of the helmet, were like two dark holes in a tree. My heart was pounding, filling my chest with pain. Still, neither of us moved. Then, almost the same instant, the guard screamed and I roared like a bull gone mad to drive him off. He let go of the sword and tried to retreat, walking backward, but he tripped on the dog and fell. I laughed, a little wild, and reached out fast as a striking snake for his leg. In a second I was on my feet again. He screamed, dangling, and then there were others all around me. They threw javelins and axes, and one of the men caught the guard's thrashing arms and tried to yank him free. I held on, but except for that I couldn't act. It was as if I too was drunk on mead. I saw their weapons come flying straight at me, saw them touch my fur and drop quietly in the grass.

Then, little by little, I understood. I felt laughter welling up inside me—at the dragon-charm, at Hrothgar's whispering and trembling by the meadhall door, at everything—the oblivious trees and sky, the witless moon. I'd meant them no harm, but they'd attacked me again, as always. They were crazy. And now at last the grim laughter came pouring out, as uncontrollable as the dragon's laugh, and I wanted to say, "Lo, God has vanquished mine enemies!"—but that made me laugh harder, though even now my heart raced and, in spite of it all, I was afraid of them. I backed away, still holding the screaming guard. They merely stared, with their useless weapons drawn, their shoulders hunched against my laughter. When I'd reached a safe distance, I held up the guard to taunt them, then held him still higher and leered into his face. He went silent, looking at me upside-down in horror, suddenly knowing what I planned. As if casually, in plain sight of them all, I bit his head off, crunched through the helmet and skull with my teeth and, holding the jerking, blood-slippery body in two hands, sucked the blood that sprayed like a hot, thick geyser from his neck. It got all over me. Women fainted, men backed toward the hall. I fled with the body to the woods, heart churning—boiling like a flooded ditch—with glee.

Some three or four nights later I launched my first raid. I burst in when they were all asleep, snatched seven from their beds, and slit them open and devoured them on the spot. I felt a strange, unearthly joy. It was as if I'd made some incredible discovery, like my discovery long ago of the moonlit world beyond the mere. I was transformed. I was a new focus for the clutter of space I stood in: if the world had once imploded on the tree where I waited, trapped and full of pain, it now blasted outward, away from me, screeching terror. I had become, myself, the mama I'd searched the cliffs for once in vain. But that merely hints at what I mean. I had *become* something, as if born again. I had hung between possibilities before, between the cold truths I knew and the heart-sucking conjuring tricks of the Shaper; now that was passed: I was Grendel, Ruiner of Meadhalls, Wrecker of Kings!

But also, as never before, I was alone.

I do not complain of it (talking talking, complaining complaining, filling the world I walk with words). But I admit it was a jolt. It was a few raids later. The meadhall door burst open at my touch exactly as before, and, for once, that night, I hesitated. Men sat up in their beds, snatched their helmets, swords, and shields from the covers beside them, and, shouting brave words that came out like squeals, they threw their legs over the sides to stumble toward me. Someone yelled, "Remember this hour, ye thanes of Hrothgar, the boasts you made as the meadbowl passed! Remember our good king's gift of rings and pay him with all your might for his many kindnesses!"

Damned pompous fools. I hurled a bench at the closest. They all cowered back. I stood waiting, bent forward with my feet apart, flat-footed, till they ended their interminable orations. I was hunched like a wrestler, moving my head from side to side, making sure no sneak slipped up on me. I was afraid of them from habit, and as the four or five drunkest of the thanes came toward me, shaking their weapons and shouting at me, my idiotic fear of them mounted. But I held my ground. Then, with a howl, one plunged at me, sword above his head in both fists. I let it come. The charm held good. I closed my hand on the blade and snatched it from the drunken thane's hand and hurled it the length of the hall. It clattered on the fireplace stones and fell to the stone floor, ringing. I seized him and crushed him. Another one came at me, gloating in his blear-eyed heroism, maniacally joyful because he had bragged that he would die for his king and he was doing it. He did it. Another came, reeling and whooping, trying to make his eyes focus.

I laughed. It was outrageous: they came, they fell, howling insanity about brothers, fathers, glorious Hrothgar, and God. But though I laughed, I felt trapped, as hollow as a rotten tree. The meadhall seemed to stretch for miles, out to the edges of time and space, and I saw myself killing them, on and on and on, as if mechanically, without contest. I saw myself swelling like bellows on their blood, a meaningless smudge in a universe dead as old wind over bones, abandoned except for the burnt-blood scent of the dragon.

All at once I began to smash things—benches, tables, hanging beds—a rage as meaningless and terrible as everything else.

Then—as a crowning absurdity, my salvation that moment—came the man the thanes called Unferth.

He stood across the hall from me, youthful, intense, cold sober. He was taller than the others; he stood out among his fellow thanes like a horse in a herd of cows. His nose was as porous and dark as volcanic rock. His light beard grew in patches.

"Stand back," he said.

The drunken little men around me backed away. The hallfloor between us, Unferth and myself, lay open.

"Monster, prepare to die!" he said. Very righteous. The wings of his nostrils flared and quivered like an outraged priest's.

I laughed. "Aargh!" I said. I spit bits of bone.

He glanced behind him, making sure he knew exactly where the window was. "Are you right with your god?" he said.

I laughed somewhat more fiercely. He was one of those.

He took a tentative step toward me, then paused, holding his sword out and shaking it. "Tell them in Hell that Unferth, son of Ecglaf sent you, known far and wide in these Scanian lands as hero among the Scyldings." He took a few sidesteps, like one wrestler circling another, except that he was thirty feet away; the maneuver was ridiculous.

"Come, come," I said. "Let me tell them I was sent by Sideways-Walker."

He frowned, trying to puzzle out my speech. I said it again, louder and slower, and a startled look came over him. Even now he didn't know what I was saying, but it was clear to him, I think, that I was speaking words. He got a cunning look, as if getting ready to offer a deal—the look men have when they fight with men instead of poor stupid animals.

He was shaken, and to get back his nerve he spoke some more. "For many months, unsightly monster, you've murdered men as you pleased in Hrothgar's hall. Unless you can murder me as you've murdered lesser men, I give you my word those days are done forever! The king has given me splendid gifts. He will see tonight that his gifts have not gone for nothing! Prepare to fall, foul thing! This one red hour makes your reputation or mine!"

I shook my head at him, wickedly smiling. "Reputation!" I said, pretending to be much impressed.

His eyebrows shot up. He'd understood me; no doubt of it now. "You can talk!" he said. He backed away a step.

I nodded, moving in on him. Near the center of the room there was a trestle table piled with glossy apples. An evil idea came over me—so evil it made me shiver as I smiled—and I sidled across to the table. "So you're a hero," I said. He didn't get it, and I said it twice more before I gave up in disgust. I talked on anyway, let him get what he could, come try for reputation when he pleased. "I'm impressed," I said. "I've never seen a live hero before. I thought they were only in poetry. Ah, ah, it must be a terrible burden, though, being a hero—glory reaper, harvester of monsters! Everybody always watching

you, weighing you, seeing if you're still heroic.
You know how it is—he he! Sooner or later the
harvest virgin will make her mistake in the hay-
stack." I laughed.

The dragon-scent in the room grew stronger,
as if my teasing were bringing the old beast near.
I picked up an apple and polished it lightly and
quickly on the hair of my arm. I had my head
bowed, smiling, looking at him up through my
eyebrows.

"Dread creature—" he said.

I went on polishing the apple, smiling. "And
the awful inconvenience," I said. "Always having
to stand erect, always having to find noble language! It must wear on a man."

He looked hurt and slightly indignant. He'd
understood.

"Wretched shape—" he said.

"But no doubt there are compensations," I
said. "The pleasant feeling of vast superiority, the
easy success with women—"

"Monster!" he howled.

"And the joy of self-knowledge, that's a
great compensation! The easy and absolute cer-
tainty that whatever the danger, however terrible
the odds, you'll stand firm, behave with the dignity of a hero, yea, even to the grave!"

"No more talk!" he yelled. His voice broke.
He lifted his sword to make a run at me, and I
laughed—howled—and threw an apple at him.
He dodged, and then his mouth dropped open. I
laughed harder, threw another. He dodged again.

"Hey!" he yelled. A forgivable lapse.

And now I was raining apples at him and
laughing myself weak. He covered his head,

roaring at me. He tried to charge through the barrage, but he couldn't make three feet. I slammed one straight into his pock-marked nose, and blood splurted out like joining rivers. It made the floor slippery, and he went down. *Clang!* I bent double with laughter. Poor Jangler—Unferth—tried to take advantage of it, charging me on all fours, snatching at my ankles, but I jumped back and tipped over the table on him, half burying him in apples as red and innocent as smiles. He screamed and thrashed, trying to get at me and at the same time trying to see if the others were watching. He was crying, only a boy, famous hero or not: a poor miserable virgin.

"Such is life," I said, and mocked a sigh. "Such is dignity!" Then I left him. I got more pleasure from that apple fight than from any other battle in my life.

I was sure, going back to my cave (it was nearly dawn), that he wouldn't follow. They never did. But I was wrong; he was a new kind of Scylding. He must have started tracking me that same morning. A driven man, a maniac. He arrived at the cave three nights later.

I was asleep. I woke up with a start, not sure what it was that had awakened me. I saw my mother moving slowly and silently past me, blue murder in her eyes. I understood instantly, not with my mind but with something quicker, and I darted around in front to block her way. I pushed her back.

There he lay, gasping on his belly like a half drowned rat. His face and throat and arms were a crosshatch of festering cuts, the leavings of the firesnakes. His hair and beard hung straight down like seaweed. He panted for a long time, then rolled his eyes up, vaguely in my direction. In the darkness he couldn't see me, though I could see him. He closed his hand on the sword hilt and jiggled the sword a little, too weak to raise it off the floor.

"Unferth has come!" he said.

I smiled. My mother moved back and forth like a bear behind me, stirred up by the smell.

He crawled toward me, the sword noisily scraping on the cave's rock floor. Then he gave out again. "It will be sung," he whispered, then paused again to get wind. "It will be sung year on year and age on age that Unferth went down through the burning lake—" he paused to pant "—and gave his life in battle with the world-rim monster." He let his cheek fall to the floor and lay panting for a long time, saying nothing. It dawned on me that he was waiting for me to kill him. I did nothing. I sat down and put my elbows on my knees and my chin on my fists and merely watched. He lay with his eyes closed and began to get his breath back. He whispered: "It's all very well to make a fool of me before my fellow thanes. All very well to talk about dignity and noble language and all the rest, as if heroism were a golden trinket, mere outward show, and hollow. But such is not the case, monster. That is to say—" He paused, seemed to grope; he'd lost his train of thought.

I said nothing, merely waited, blocking my mother by stretching out an arm when she came near.

"Even now you mock me," Unferth whispered. I had an uneasy feeling he was close to tears. If he wept, I was not sure I could control myself. His pretensions to uncommon glory were one thing. If for even an instant he pretended to misery like mine . . .

"You think me a witless fool," he whispered. "Oh, I heard what you said. I caught your nasty insinuations. 'I thought heroes were only in poetry,' you said. Implying that what I've made of myself is mere fairytale stuff." He raised his head, trying to glare at me, but his blind stare was in the wrong direction, following my mother's pacing. "Well, it's not, let me tell you." His lips trembled and I was certain he would cry, I would have to destroy him from pure disgust, but he held it. He let his head fall again and sucked for air. A little of his voice came back, so that he no longer had to whisper but could bring out his words in a slightly reedy whine. "Poetry's trash, mere clouds of words, comfort to the hopeless. But this is no cloud, no syllabled phantom that stands here shaking its sword at you."

I let the slight exaggeration pass.

But Unferth didn't. "Or lies here," he said. "A hero is not afraid to face cruel truth." That reminded him, apparently, of what he'd meant to say before. "You talk of heroism as noble language, dignity. It's more than that, as my coming here has proved. No man above us will ever know whether Unferth died here or fled to the hills like a coward. Only you and I and God will know the truth. That's inner heroism."

"Hmm," I said. It was not unusual, of course, to hear them contradict themselves, but I would have liked it if he'd stuck to one single version, either that they would know and sing his tragedy or that they wouldn't. So it would have been in a poem, surely, if Unferth were a character, good or evil, heroic or not. But reality, alas, is essentially shoddy. I let out a sigh.

He jerked his head up, shocked. "Does *nothing* have value in your horrible ruin of a brain?"

I waited. The whole shit-ass scene was his idea, not mine.

I saw the light dawning in his eyes. "I understand," he said. I thought he would laugh at the bottomless stupidity of my cynicism, but while the laugh was still starting at the corners of his eyes, another look came, close to fright. "You think me deluded. Tricked by my own walking fairytale. You think I came without a hope of winning—came to escape indignity by suicide!" He did laugh now, not amused: sorrowful and angry. The laugh died quickly. "I didn't know how deep the pool was," he said. "I had a chance. I knew I had no more than that. It's all a hero asks for."

I sighed. The word "hero" was beginning to grate. He was an idiot. I could crush him like a fly, but I held back.

"Go ahead, scoff," he said, petulant. "Except in the life of a hero, the whole world's meaningless. The hero sees values beyond what's possible. That's the *nature* of a hero. It kills him, of course, ultimately. But it makes the whole struggle of humanity worthwhile."

I nodded in the darkness. "And breaks up the boredom," I said.

He raised up on his elbows, and the effort of it made his shoulders shake. "One of us is going to die tonight. Does *that* break up your boredom?"

"It's not true," I said. "A few minutes from now I'm going to carry you back to Hrothgar, safe and sound. So much for poetry."

"I'll kill myself," he whispered. He shook violently now.

"Up to you," I answered reasonably, "but you'll admit it may seem at least a trifle cowardly to some."

His fists closed and his teeth clenched; then he relaxed and lay flat.

I waited for him to find an answer. Minutes passed. It came to me that he had quit. He had glimpsed a glorious ideal, had struggled toward it and seized it and come to understand it, and was disappointed. One could sympathize.

He was asleep.

I picked him up gently and carried him home. I laid him at the door of Hrothgar's meadhall, still asleep, killed the two guards so I wouldn't be misunderstood, and left.

He lives on, bitter, feebly challenging my midnight raids from time to time (three times this summer), crazy with shame that he alone is always spared, and furiously jealous of the dead. I laugh when I see him. He throws himself at me, or he cunningly sneaks up behind, sometimes in disguise—a goat, a dog, a sickly old woman—and I roll on the floor with laughter. So much for heroism. So much for the harvest-virgin. So much, also, for the alternative visions of blind old poets and dragons.

7

Balance is everything, riding out time like a helm-less sheepboat, keel to hellward, mast upreared to prick out heaven's eye. He he! (Sigh.) My enemies define themselves (as the dragon said) on me. As for myself, I could finish them off in a single night, pull down the great carved beams and crush them in the meadhall, along with their mice, their tank-ards and potatoes—yet I hold back. I am hardly blind to the absurdity. Form is function. What will we call the Hrothgar-Wrecker when Hrothgar has been wrecked?

(Do a little dance, beast. Shrug it off. This looks like a nice place—oooh, my!—flat rock, moonlight, views of distances! Sing!

> Pity poor Hrothgar,
> Grendel's foe!
> Pity poor Grendel,
> O, O, O!

Winter soon.
(whispering, whispering. Grendel, has it oc-curred to you my dear that you are crazy?)

(He clasps hands delicately over his head, points the toes of one foot—*aaie!* horrible nails!!—takes a step, does a turn:

> *Grendel is crazy,*
> *O, O, O!*
> *Thinks old Hrothgar*
> *Makes it snow!*

Balance is everything, tiding out rhyme . . .

> *Pity poor Grengar,*
> *Hrothdel's foe!*
> *Down goes the whirlpool:*
> *Eek! No, no!*

It will be winter soon.
Midway through the twelfth year of my idiotic war.
Twelve is, I hope, a holy number. Number of escapes from traps.
[*He searches the moonlit world for signs, shading his eyes against the dimness, standing on one shaggy foot, just slightly bloodstained, one toe missing from an old encounter with an ax. Three dead trees on the moor below, burned up alive by lightning, are ominous portents. (Oh man, us portents!) Also trees. On a frostbitten hill in the distance, men on horses. "Over here!" he screams. Waves his arms. They hesitate, feign deafness, ride away north. Shoddy, he observes. The whole chilly universe, shoddy.*]

Enough of that! A night for tearing heads off, bathing in blood! Except, alas, he has killed his quota for the season. Care, take care of the gold-egg-laying goose! There is no limit to desire but desire's needs. (Grendel's law.)

The scent of the dragon. Heavy all around me, almost visible before me, like my breath.

I will count my numberless blessings one by one.

1. My teeth are sound.
1. The roof of my cave is sound.
1. I have not committed the ultimate act of nihilism: I have not killed the queen.
1. Yet.

(*He lies on the cliff-edge, scratching his belly, and thoughtfully watches his thoughtfully watching the queen.*)

Not easy to define. Mathematically, perhaps a torus, loosely cylindrical, with swellings and constrictions at intervals, knobbed—that is to say, a surface generated, more or less, by the revolutions of a conic about an axis lying in its plane, and the solid thus enclosed. It is difficult, of course, to be precise. For one thing, the problem of determining how much is queen and how much queenly radiation.

The monster laughs.

Time-Space cross-section: *Wealtheow.*

Cut *A:*

It was the second year of my raiding. The army of the Scyldings was weakened, decimated. No more the rumble of Hrothgar's horsemen, riding at midnight, chain-mail jangling in the whistling wind, cloaks flying out like wimpling wings, to rescue petty tribute-givers. (O *listen* to me, hills!) He couldn't protect his own hall, much less theirs. I cut down my visits, conserving the game, and watched them. Nature lover. For weeks, all day and far into the night, he met with his counselors, talking, praying, moaning. I became aware, listening to them, that I was not their only threat. Far to the east of Hrothgar's hall there was a new hall a-building, its young king gaining fame. As Hrothgar had done, this younger king was systematically burning and plundering nearby halls, extending the circle of his tribute power. He was striking now at the outer rim of Hrothgar's sphere; it was only a matter of time before he struck Hrothgar. The counselors talked and drank and wept, sometimes Hrothgar's allies among them. The Shaper sang songs. The men stood with their braceleted arms around one another's shoulders—men who not long before had been the bitterest of enemies—and I watched it all, wringing my fingers, smiling rage. The leaves turned red. The purple blooms of thistles became black behind the people's houses, and migrant birds moved through.

Then, from all corners of Hrothgar's sphere of influence and from towns beyond—the vassals' vassals—an army began to form. They came walking or riding, oxen dragging their wagonloads of shields, spears, tents, clothes, food. Every night when I went down to look there were more of them. Cartwheels tall as a man, with rough, square spokes. Big-hoofed gray horses spackled like wolves, that rolled their eyes and whinnied at my footfall, leagued with men as if strapped to their business by harnesses I could not see. Horns cracked out in the darkening stillness; grindstones screeched. The crisp air reeked with the aftersmell of their cooking.

They made camp in a sloping pasture rimmed by enormous oak trees and pines and nut trees, a stream moving down through the center, over steps of rock. Where the forest began, there was a lake. Every night there were new groups of campfires to push away the frost, and soon there was hardly a place to stand, there were so many men and animals. The grass, the withering leaves were full of whispering, but the campground was hushed, muffled by their presence, as if blighted. I watched from my hiding place. They talked in mumbles or not at all. Message carriers moved from fire to fire, talking softly with the leaders. Their rich furs shone like birds' wings in the firelight. Heavily guarded, the younger soldiers pushed through the crowd and, all night long, washed clothes and cooking ware in the stream until the water was thick with dirt and grease and no longer made a sound as it dropped toward the lake. When they slept, guards and dogs watched over them in herds. Before dawn, men rose to exercise the horses, polish weapons, or move out with bows in search of deer.

Then one night when I went down to spy, they were gone, vanished like starlings from a tree. I followed their trail—footprints, hoofprints, and wagon ruts cutting a wide dirty swath toward the east. When I came in sight of them, I slowed down, laughing and hugging myself; it was going to be a massacre. They marched all night, then scattered into the forest like wolves and slept all day without fires. I snatched an ox and devoured it, leaving no trace. At dusk, they formed again. At midnight the armies arrived at the antlered hall.

Hrothgar called out to him, glorious protector of the Scyldings, hoarfrost bearded: "Hygmod, lord of the Helmings, greet your guests!" Unferth stood beside him, his huge arms folded on his byrnie. He stood with his head bowed, eyes mere slits, clamped mouth hidden where his mustache overlapped his beard. Bitterness went out from him like darkness made visible: Unferth the hero (known far and wide in these Scanian lands), isolated in that huge crowd like a poisonous snake aware of what it was. King Hrothgar called again.

The young king came out, well armed, leading a bear and six retainers. He looked around him, blond and pale, arms ringed with gold, a vague smile hiding his shock. The army of the Scyldings and all their allies stretched off in the darkness as far as the eye could see—down the slopes of the hill, down the stone-paved roadways, away into the trees.

Hrothgar made a speech, lifting his ashspear and shaking it. The young man waited like stone, his gloved right hand grasping the chain that led the bear. He had no chance, and he knew it. Everyone knew it but the bear beside him, standing upright, considering the crowd. I smiled. I could smell the blood that would drench the ground before morning came. There was a light breeze, a scent of winter in it. It stirred the fur on the men's clothes and rattled the leaves around me. The bear dropped down on all fours and grunted. The king jerked the chain. Then an old man came out of the mead-hall, went to the young king, just clear of the bear, and spoke to him. Hrothgar and all his allies were silent, waiting. The young king and the old man talked. The retainers at the meadhall door joined in, their voices low. I waited. Hrothgar's whole army was silent. Then the young king moved toward Hrothgar. A rumble went through the crowd, then fell away like a wave retreating, drawing pebbles out from shore. At last, very slowly, the young king drew out his sword, with his left hand—a sign of truce—and dropped it, as if casually, in front of Hrothgar's horse.

"We will give you gifts," the young king said, "splendid tribute in sign of our great respect for the honorable Scyldings." His voice and smile were gracious. His eyes, slanting downward like the eyes of a fish, were expressionless as dried-up wells.

Unferth laughed, all alone in the silence. The sound rolled away to the darkness to die among trees.

Hrothgar, white-haired, white-bearded as the ice-god, shook his head. "There is no gift your people can give the Scyldings," he said. "You think you can buy a little time with gold, and then some night when we're sitting at our mead, you and all your brave allies will come down on us—crash!— as we tonight have come down on you, and no gift we can offer then will turn away your fury." The old man smiled, his eyes wicked. "Do you take us for children that play in the yards with pets? What could we give you that you couldn't take by force, and at that time take from us ten-fold?"

Unferth smiled, looking at the bear. The young king showed nothing, accepting the joke and the argument as if he'd been expecting them. He gave the chain another jerk and the bear moved closer to him. When he'd waited long enough, he looked back up at Hrothgar.

"We can give you such piles of treasure," he said, "that I have nothing left to pay an army with. Then you'll be safe."

Hrothgar laughed. "You're crafty, lord of the Helmings. A king shrewd with words can mount a great army on promises. The treasure you'd take by destroying my house could make all your swordsmen rich. Come, come! No more talk! It's a chilly night, and we have cows to milk in the morning. Take up your weapons. We'll give you ground. We haven't come to kill you like foxes in a hole."

But the young king waited on. He was still smiling, though his eyes had no life in them. He had something in reserve, some ingenious product of his counselor's wits that would overwhelm their scheme. He said, speaking more quietly than before, "I will show you a treasure that will change your mind, great Hrothgar." He turned to an attendant and made a sign. The attendant went into the meadhall.

After a long time he returned. He was carrying nothing. Behind him, men opened the meadhall door wide. Light burst over the hillside and glinted on the weapons and eyes of the Scyldings. The bear stirred, restless, irritable, like the young king's anger removed to the end of a chain. Old Hrothgar waited.

Then at last, moving slowly, as if walking in a dream, a woman in a robe of threaded silver came gliding from the hall. Her smooth long hair was as red as fire and soft as the ruddy sheen on dragon's gold. Her face was gentle, mysteriously calm. The night became more still.

"I offer you my sister," the young king said. "Let her name from now on be Wealtheow, or holy servant of common good."

I leered in the rattling darkness of my tree. The name was ridiculous. "Pompous, pompous ass!" I hissed. But she was beautiful and she surrendered herself with the dignity of a sacrificial virgin. My chest was full of pain, my eyes smarted, and I was afraid—O monstrous trick against reason—I was afraid I was about to sob. I wanted to smash things, bring down the night with my howl of rage. But I kept still. She was beautiful, as innocent as dawn on winter hills. She tore me apart as once the Shaper's song had done. As if for my benefit, as if in vicious scorn of me, children came from the mead-hall and ran down to her, weeping, to snatch at her hands and dress.

"Stop it!" I whispered. "Stupid!"

She did not look at them, merely touched their heads. "Be still," she said—hardly more than a whisper, but it carried across the crowd. They were still, as if her voice were magic. I clenched my teeth, tears streaming from my eyes. She was like a child, her sweet face paler than the moon. She looked up at Hrothgar's beard, not his eyes, afraid of him. "My lord," she said.

O woe! O wretched violation of sense!

I could see myself leaping from my high tree and running on all fours through the crowd to her, howling, whimpering, throwing myself down, drooling and groveling at her small, fur-booted feet. "Mercy!" I would howl. "Aargh! Burble!" I clamped my palms over my eyes and struggled not to laugh.

No need to say more. The old king accepted the younger king's gift, along with some other things—swords and cups, some girls and young men, her servants. For several days both sides made speeches, long-winded, tediously poetic, all lies, and then, with much soft weeping and sniffling, the Scyldings loaded up Wealtheow and the lesser beauties, made a few last touching observations, and went home.

A bad winter. I couldn't lay a hand on them, prevented as if by a charm. I huddled in my cave, grinding my teeth, beating my forehead with my fists and cursing nature. Sometimes I went up to the frozen cliffwall and looked down, down, at where the lights lay blue, like the threads running out from a star, patterning the snow. My fists struck out at the cliff's ice-crusted rock. It was no satisfaction. In the cave again, I listened to my mother move back and forth, a pale shape driven by restlessness and rage at the restlessness and rage she felt in me and could not cure. She would gladly have given her life to end my suffering— horrible, humpbacked, carp-toothed creature, eyes on fire with useless, mindless love. Who could miss the grim parallel? So the lady below would give, had given, her life for those she loved. So would any simpering, eyelash-batting female in her court, given the proper setup, the minimal conditions. The smell of the dragon lay around me like sulphurous smoke. At times I would wake up in panic, unable to breathe.

At times I went down.

She carried the mealbowl from table to table, smiling quietly, as if the people she served, her husband's people, were her own. The old king watched with thoughtful eyes, moved as he'd have been by the Shaper's music, except that it was different: not visions of glorious things that might be or sly revisions of the bloody past but present beauty that made time's flow seem illusory, some lower law that now had been suspended. Meaning as quality. When drunken men argued, pitting theory against theory, bludgeoning each other's absurdities, she came between them, wordless, un-condemning, pouring out mead like a mother's love, and they were softened, reminded of their humanness, exactly as they might have been soft-ened by the cry of a child in danger, or an old

man's suffering, or spring. The Shaper sang things
that had never crossed his mind before: comfort,
beauty, a wisdom softer, more permanent, than
Hrothgar's. The old king watched, remote from the
queen, though she shared his bed, and he mused.

One night she paused in front of Unferth. He sat
hunched, bitterly smiling, as always, his muscles
taut as old nautical ropes in a hurricane. He was
ugly as a spider.

"My lord?" she said. She often called the thanes
"my lord." Servant of even the lowliest among
them.

"No thank you," he said. He shot a glance at
her, then looked down, smiled fiercely. She waited,
expressionless except for perhaps the barest trace of
puzzlement. He said, "I've had enough."

Down the table a man made bold by mead said,
"Men have been known to kill their brothers when
they've too much mead. Har, har."

A few men laughed.

Unferth stiffened. The queen's face paled. Once
again Unferth glanced up at the queen, then away.
His fists closed tight, resting on the table in front
of him, inches from his knife. No one moved. The
hall became still. She stood strange-eyed, as if looking out from another world and time. Who can
say what she understood? I knew, for one, that
the brother-killer had put on the Shaper's idea of
the hero like a merry mask, had seen it torn away,
and was now reduced to what he was: a thinking
animal stripped naked of former illusions, stubbornly living on, ashamed and meaningless, because killing himself would be, like his life,
unheroic. It was a paradox nothing could resolve
but a murderous snicker. The moment stretched,
a snag in time's stream, and still no one moved, no

one spoke. As if defiantly, Unferth, murderer of brothers, again raised his eyes to the queen's, and this time didn't look down. Scorn? Shame?

The queen smiled. Impossibly, like roses blooming in the heart of December, she said, "That's past." And it was. The demon was exorcised. I saw his hands unclench, relax, and—torn between tears and a bellow of scorn—I crept back to my cave.

It was not, understand, that she had secret wells of joy that overflowed to them all. She lay beside the sleeping king—I watched wherever she went, a crafty guardian, wealthy in wiles—and her eyes were open, the lashes bright with tears. She was more child, those moments, than woman. Thinking of home, remembering paths in the land of the Helmings where she'd played before she'd lain aside her happiness for theirs. She held the naked, bony king as if he were the child, and nothing between him and the darkness but her white arm. Sometimes she'd slip from the bed while he slept and would cross to the door and go out alone into the night. Alone and never alone. Instantly, guards were all around her, gem-woman priceless among the Scylding treasures. She would stand in the cold wind looking east, one hand clutching her robe to her throat, the silent guards encircling her like trees. Child though she was, she would show no sign of her sorrow in front of them. At last some guard would speak to her, would mention the cold, and Wealtheow would smile and nod her thanks and go back in.

Once that winter her brother came, with his bear and a great troop of followers, to visit. Their talk and laughter rumbled up to the cliffwall. The double band drank, the Shaper sang, and then they drank again. I listened from a distance for as long as I could stand it, clenching my mind on the words of the dragon, then, helpless as always, I went down. The wind howled, piling up snow in drifts and blinding the night with ice-white dust. I walked bent over against the cold, protecting my eyes with my arms. Trees, posts, cowsheds loomed into my vision, then vanished, swallowed in white. When I came near Hart, I could smell the guards of the hall all around me, but I couldn't see them—nor, of course, could they see me. I went straight to the wall, plunging through drifts to my knees, and pressed up against it for its warmth. It trembled and shook from the noise inside. I bent down to the crack I'd used before and watched.

She was brighter than the hearthfire, talking again with her family and friends, observing the antics of the bear. It was the king, old Hrothgar, who carried the meadbowl from table to table to-night. He walked, dignified, from group to group, smiling and filling the drinking cups, and you'd have sworn from his look that never until tonight had the old man been absolutely happy. He would glance at his queen from time to time as he moved among his people and hers, the Danes and Helmings, and with each glance his smile would grow warmer for a moment, and a thoughtful look would come over his eyes. Then it would pass—some gesture or word from a guest or one of his Scylding thanes —and he would be hearty, merry: not false, exactly, but less than what he was at the moment of the glance. As for the queen, she seemed not to know he was there. She sat beside her brother, her hand on his arm, the other hand on the arm of a shriveled old woman, precious relative. The bear sat with his feet stuck out, playing with his penis and survey-ing the hall with a crotchety look, as if dimly aware that there was something about him that humans could not approve. The Helming guests all talked at once, eagerly, constantly, as if squeezing all their past into an evening. I couldn't hear what they said. The hall was a roar—voices, the clink of cups, the shuffle of feet. Sometimes Wealtheow would tip back her head, letting her copper-red hair fall free, and laugh; sometimes she listened, head cocked, now smiling, now soberly pursing her lips, only offering a nod. Hrothgar went back to his high, carved chair, relinquishing the bowl to the noblest of his thanes, and sat like an old man listening inside his mind to the voices of his childhood. Once, for a long moment, the queen looked at him while listening to her brother, her eyes as thoughtful as Hrothgar's. Then she laughed and talked again, and the king conversed with the man on his left; it was as if their minds had not met.

Later that night they passed a harp—not the old Shaper's instrument, no one touched that—and the queen's brother sang. He was no artist, with either his fingers or his throat, but all the hall was silent, listening. He sang, childlike except for the winter in his gray eyes, of a hero who'd killed a girl's old father out of love of the girl, and how the girl after that had both loved and hated the hero and finally had killed him. Wealtheow smiled, full of sorrow, as she listened. The bear irritably watched the dogs. Then others sang. Old Hrothgar watched and listened, brooding on dangers. (The queen's brother had straw-yellow hair and eyes as gray as slate. Sometimes when he stole a glance at Hrothgar, his face was a knife.)

Toward morning, they all went to bed. Half buried in snow, the deadly cold coming up through my feet, I kept watch. The queen put her hand on

Hrothgar's bare shoulder as he slept and looked at him thoughtfully, exactly as Hrothgar had looked at her and at his people. She moved a strand of hair from his face. After a long, long time she closed her eyes, but even now I wasn't sure she was asleep.

And so in my cave, coughing from the smoke and clenching feet on fire with chilblains, I ground my teeth on my own absurdity. Whatever their excuse might be, I had none, I knew: I had seen the dragon. Ashes to ashes. And yet I was teased— tortured by the red of her hair and the set of her chin and the white of her shoulders—teased to- ward disbelief in the dragon's truths. A glorious moment was coming, my chest insisted, and even the fact that I myself would have no part in it—a member of the race God cursed, acording to the Shaper's tale—was trifling. In my mind I watched her freckled hand move on the old man's arm as once I'd listened to the sigh of the Shaper's harp. Ah, woe, woe! How many times must a creature be dragged down the same ridiculous road? The Shaper's lies, the hero's self-delusion, now this: the idea of a queen! My mother, breathing hard, scraping through her hair with her crooked nails, watched me and sometimes moaned.

And so, the next night—it was dark as pitch—I burst the meadhall door, killed men, and stormed directly to the door behind which lay the sleeping queen. Glorious Unferth slept beside it. He rose to fight me. I slapped him aside like a troublesome colt. The queen's brother rose, unleashed the bear. I accepted its hug in my own and broke its back. I slammed into the bedroom. She sat up screaming, and I laughed. I snatched her foot, and now her

unqueenly shrieks were deafening, exactly like the
squeals of a pig. No one would defend her, not
even suicidal Unferth at the door, screaming his
rage—self-hatred. Old Hrothgar shook and made
lunatic noises and drooled. I could have jerked her
from the bed and stove in her golden-haired head
against the wall. They watched in horror, Helmings on one side, Scyldings on the other (balance is
anything), and I caught the other foot and pulled
her naked legs apart as if to split her. "Gods, gods!"
she screamed. I waited to see if the gods would
come, but not a sign of them. I laughed. She called
to her brother, then Unferth. They hung back. I
decided to kill her. I firmly committed myself to
killing her, slowly, horribly. I would begin by
holding her over the fire and cooking the ugly
hole between her legs. I laughed harder at that.
They were all screaming now, hooting and yawling
to their dead-stick gods. I would kill her, yes! I
would squeeze out her feces between my fists. So
much for meaning as quality of life! I would kill
her and teach them reality. Grendel the truth-
teacher, phantasm-tester! It was what I would be
from this day forward—my commitment, my
character as long as I lived—and nothing alive or
dead could change my mind!

I changed my mind. It would be meaningless,
killing her. As meaningless as letting her live. It
would be, for me, mere pointless pleasure, an illusion of order for this one frail, foolish flicker-
flash in the long dull fall of eternity. (End quote.)

I let go her feet. The people stared, unbelieving.
I had wrecked another theory. I left the hall.

But I'd cured myself. That much, at least, I could
say for my behavior. I concentrated on the memory
of the ugliness between her legs (bright tears of

blood) and laughed as I ran through the heavy snow. The night was still. I could hear their crying in the meadhall. "Ah, Grendel, you sly old devil!" I whispered to the trees. The words rang false. (The east was gray.) I hung balanced, a creature of two minds; and one of them said—unreasonable, stubborn as the mountains—that she was beautiful. I resolved, absolutely and finally, to kill myself, for love of the Baby Grendel that used to be. But the next instant, for no particular reason, I changed my mind.

Balance is everything, sliding down slime. . . . Cut *B*.

8

After the murder of Halga the Good,
dear younger brother of bold king Hrothgar
(helm of the Scyldings, sword-hilt handler,
bribe-gold bender who by his wife had
now two sons) came Hrothulf out of
orphan's woe to Hart.

               (O hear me,
rocks and trees, loud waterfalls! You imagine I tell
you these things just to hear myself speak? A little
respect there, brothers and sisters!

    (Thus poor Grendel,
    anger's child,
    red eyes hidden in the dark of verbs,
    brachiating with a hoot from rhyme to rhyme.)

       SCENE: *The Arrival of Hrothulf at Hart.*

"Hrothulf! Come to Aunt Wealtheow!
You poor, poor dear boy!"
"It is very kind of you, madam, to take me in."

"Nonsense, dearest! You're Hrothgar's flesh and
    blood!"

"So I'm told." A mumble. Trace of smile.

The old king frowns in his carved chair.

The boy has the manners, he broods, of a half-
    tamed wolf.

Fourteen years old and already a God-damned
    pretender?

Age, old chain of victories, where is your comfort?

He clears his throat.

No no; I jump to conclusions.

The boy has been through a bad time,

naturally. Father-funeral and all the rest.

And gifted, of course, with a proud heart,

like all his line. (Oft Scyld Shefing . . .)

(The hawk in the rafters hands down no opinion.)

The Shaper sings—the harp soughing out through
    the long room

like summer wind—"By deeds worth praise

a man can, in any kingdom, prosper!"

So.

The boy sits solemn and hears the harp

behind closed eyes. The October hills in his calm

mind run wolves.

Theorum: Any action (*A*) of the human heart

must trigger an equal and opposite reaction (A^1).

Such is the golden opinion of the Shaper.

And so—I watch in glee—they take in Hrothulf;

quiet as the moon, sweet scorpion,

he sits between their two and cleans his knife.

SCENE: *Hrothulf in the Yard.*
      Hrothulf speaks:

In ratty furs the peasants hoe their fields,

fat with stupidity, if not with flesh. Their foodsmells
foul the doorways, dungeon dark, where cow-eyed
   girls
give tit to the next generation's mindless hoe.
   Old men
with ringworm in their beards limp dusty lanes
to gather like bony dogs at the god-lined square
where the king's justice is dispensed; to nod like
   crows
at slips of the tongue by which a horse
   is lost, or delicate mistakes
of venue through which murderers run free.
   "Long live
the king!" they squeak, "to whom we owe all joy!"
Obese with imagined freedom if not with fat,
   great lords
of lords look down with cowdog eyes and smile.
"All's well," they sigh. "Long live the king! All's
   well!"
Law rules the land. Men's violence is chained
to good (i.e., to the king): legitimate force
that chops the bread-thief's neck and wipes its
   ax.—Death
by book.
      Think, sweating beast! Look up and think!
Whence came these furs on the backs of your kind
   protectors?
Why does the bread-thief die and the murdering
   thane
escape by a sleight by the costliest of advocates?
Think! Squeeze up your wrinkled face
and seize the hangnail tip of a searing thought:
*Violence hacked this shack-filled hole in the woods
   where you*
*play freedom games. Violence no more legitimate
   then*

than a wolf's. And now by violence they lock
us in—you and me, old man: subdue our vile
unkingly violence. Come into the shade.
I would have a word with you and your wart-hog
  son.

SCENE: *Hrothulf in the Woods.*

The nut tree, wide above my head,
stretching its cool black limbs to take
the sun, sends darkness down my chest.
Its dappled, highcrowned roadways make
safe homes for birds; quick squirrels run
the veins of its treasure-giving hand;
but the ground below is dead.

Strange providence! Shall I call the tree
tyrannical, since where it stands
nothing survives but itself and its high-
borne guests? Condemn it because it sends
down stifling darkness, sucks the life
from grass, and whitens the sapling leaf
for trifling, fluttering friends?

The law of the world is a winter law,
and casual. I too can be grim:
snatch my daylight by violent will
and be glorified for the deed, like him;
drain my soil of Considerations,
grip my desires like underground stones,
let old things sicken and fail.

She touches my hair and smiles, kind,
trusting the rhetoric of love: Give
and get. But the thought flits through my mind,

There have got to be stabler things than love.
The blurred tree towering overhead
consumes the sun; the ground is dead;
I gasp for rain and wind.

SCENE: *The Queen Beside Hrothulf's Bed.*
Wealtheow speaks:

So sad so young? And even in sleep?
Worse times are yet to come, my love.
The babes you comfort when they weep
Will soon by birthright have

All these gold rings! Ah, then, then
Your almost-brother love will cool;
The cousin smile must grind out lean
Where younger cousins rule.

When I was a child I truly loved:
Unthinking love as calm and deep
As the North Sea. But I have lived,
And now I do not sleep.

In short, I watched the idea of violence growing
in him, and apprehension in all of them, and I en-
joyed myself (old hellroads-runner, earth-rim-
roamer), sucking glee from spite,—O sucking to
the pits! He hardly spoke when he first came,
skinny, pimply, beardless except for the babyhair on
his upper lip and chin. At the end of a year he
never spoke at all, unless he was forced to it or
found himself alone with the foul old old peasant he met in the woods sometimes, his counselor.
Hrothulf had hair as black as coal and hazel eyes

that never blinked. He stood, always, with his head slung forward and his lips in a pout, like a man straining to remember something. The old man—he was nicknamed Red Horse—had a perpetually startled look, round, red eyes and mouth, white hair that flared around his high, empty dome like the beams of the sun: the look of a man who has suddenly remembered something. I followed the two down shaded paths, skull-lined, since I had used them often (but our travelers did not see the skulls)—Hrothulf stumbling over roots and stones, the old man swinging along on one stiff leg. He spit when he talked, his eyes bugged. He stunk.

"To step out of the region of legality requires an extraordinary push of circumstance," the old man yelled. He was deaf and shouted as if everyone else were too. "The incitement to violence depends upon total transvaluation of the ordinary values. By a single stroke, the most criminal acts must be converted to heroic and meritorious deeds. If the Revolution comes to grief, it will be because you and those you lead have become alarmed at your own brutality."

Hrothulf fell down. The old man went on swinging along the path, oblivious, waving his fists. Hrothulf looked around him in slight surprise, understood that he had fallen, and got up. He almost fell again as he ran to catch his adviser. "Make no mistake, my beloved prince," the old man was yelling. "The total ruin of institutions and morals is an act of creation. A *religious* act. Murder and mayhem are the life and soul of revolution. I imagine you won't laugh when I tell you that. There are plenty of fools who would."

"Oh no, sir," said Hrothulf.

"The very soul! What does a kingdom pretend

to do? Save the values of the community—regulate compromise—improve the quality of the commonwealth! In other words, protect the power of the people in power and keep the others down. By common agreement of course, so the fiction goes. And they do pretty well. We'll give them that."

Hrothulf nodded. "We have to give them that."

"Rewards to people who fit the System best, you know. King's immediate thanes, the thanes' top servants, and so on till you come to the people who don't fit at all. No problem. Drive them to the darkest corners of the kingdom, starve them, throw them in jail or put them out to war."

"That's how it works."

"But satisfy the greed of the majority, and the rest will do you no harm. That's it. You've still got your fiction of consent. If the lowest of the workers start grumbling, claim that the power of the state stands above society, regulating it, moderating it, keeping it within the bounds of order—an impersonal and higher authority of justice. And what if the workers are beyond your reconciliation? Cry 'Law!' Cry 'Common good' and put on the pressure—arrest and execute a few."

"A stinking fraud," Hrothulf said, and bit his lip. There were tears in his eyes. The old serf laughed.

"Exactly, my boy! What is the state in a time of domestic or foreign crisis? What is the state when the chips are down? The answer is obvious and clear! Oh yes! If a few men quit work, the police move in. If the borders are threatened, the army rolls out. Public force is the life and soul of every state: not merely army and police but prisons, judges, tax collectors, every conceivable trick of coercive repression. The state is an organization of violence, a monopoly in what it is pleased to call *legitimate* violence. Revolution, my dear prince, is not the substitution of immoral for moral, or of illegitimate for legitimate violence; it is simply the pitting of power against power where the issue is freedom for the winners and enslavement of the rest."

Hrothulf stopped. "That's not at all what I intend," he said. "There can be more freedom or less freedom in different states."

The old man stopped too, several steps ahead of him on the forest path, and looked back, polite by an effort. "Well, that may be," he said. He shrugged.

Hrothulf, though clumsy, was no fool. He said angrily (unaware of the irony that he, a prince, had a right to anger, and the old man, a peasant, did not), "Nobody in his right mind would praise violence for its own sake, regardless of its ends!"

The old man shrugged and put on a childish smile. "But I'm a simple man, you see," he said, "and that's exactly what I do. All systems are evil. All governments are evil. Not just a trifle evil. *Monstrously* evil." Though he still smiled, he was shaking, only half controlling it. "If you want me to help you destroy a government, I'm here to serve. But as for Universal Justice—" He laughed.

Hrothulf puckered his lips, stared thoughtfully past him.

Hrothgar's nephew was kind, for all that, to the cousins he half intended to displace. He was a moody, lonely young man, after all, afraid of strangers, awkward even with the adults he knew well, and the cousins were plump blond children of three and four. There was one other cousin,

Freawaru, Hrothgar's daughter by a woman who'd died. Whenever Freawaru spoke to him, Hrothulf blushed.

He sat between the two boys at the table and helped them with their food, smiling when they talked but rarely answering. The queen would glance at the three now and then. So would others, sometimes. They all knew what was coming, though nobody believed it. Who can look into the wet-mouthed smiles of children and see a meadhall burning, or listen past their musical prattle to the midnight roar of fire?

—Except, of course, old Hrothgar. Violence and shame have lined the old man's face with mysterious calm. I can hardly look at him without a welling of confused, unpleasant emotion. He sits tall and still in his carved chair, stiff arms resting on the chair-sides, his clear eyes trained on the meadhall door where I'll arrive, if I come. When someone speaks to him, he answers politely and gently, his mind far away—on murdered thanes, abandoned hopes. He's a giant. He had in his youth the strength of seven men. Not now. He has nothing left but the power of his mind—and no pleasure there: a case of knives. The civilization he meant to build has transmogrified to a forest thick with traps. Hrothulf, he knows, is a danger to his sons; but he cannot abandon the child of his dead younger brother. Hygmod, his brother-in-law, is biding his time while Hrothgar lives, because of Wealtheow; but Hygmod, he knows, is no friend. And then there is a man named Ingeld, ruler of the Heathobards, as famous for slaughter as was Hrothgar in his day. The old man intends to deal out Freawaru to him; he has no assurance it will work. And then too there's his treasure-hoard. Another

trap. A man plunders to build up wealth to pay his
men and bring peace to the kingdom, but the hoard
he builds for his safety becomes the lure of every
marauder that happens to hear of it. Hrothgar,
keen of mind, is out of schemes. No fault of his.
There are no schemes left. And so he waits like a
man chained in a cave, staring at the entrance or,
sometimes, gazing with sad, absent-minded eyes
at Wealtheow, chained beside him. Who is one more
trap, the worst. She's young, could have served a
more vigorous man. And beautiful: need not have
withered her nights and wasted her body on a
bony, shivering wretch. She knows all this, which
increases his pain and guilt. She understands the
fear for his people that makes a coward of him, so
that, that night when I attacked her, he would not
lift a finger to preserve her. And his fear is one he
cannot even be sure is generous; perhaps mere desire that his name and fame live on. She understands too his bitterness at growing old. She even
understands—more terrible, no doubt, than all the
rest—old Hrothgar's knowledge that peace must be
searched through ordeal upon ordeal, with no final
prospect but failure. Lesson on lesson they've suf-
fered through, recognizing, more profoundly each
time, their indignity, shame, triviality. It will continue.

How, if I know all this, you may ask, could I
hound him—shatter him again and again, drive him
deeper and deeper into woe? I have no answer,
except perhaps this: why should I *not*? Has he
made any move to deserve my kindness? If I give
him a truce, will the king invite me in for a kiss on
the forehead, a cup of mead? Ha! This nobility of
his, this dignity: are they not *my* work? What was

he before? Nothing! A swollen-headed raider, full
of boasts and stupid jokes and mead. No more noble
than Red Horse, Hrothulf's friend. No one would
have balked at my persecuting him then! I made
him what he is. Have I not a right to test my own
creation? Enough! Who says I have to defend myself? I'm a machine, like you. Like all of you. Blood-
lust and rage are my character. Why does the lion
not wisely settle down and be a horse? In any case,
I too am learning, ordeal by ordeal, my indignity.
It's all I have, my only weapon for smashing
through these stiff coffin-walls of the world. So I
dance in the moonlight, make foul jokes, or labor
to shake the foundations of night with my heaped-
up howls of rage. Something is bound to come of
all this. I cannot believe such monstrous energy of
grief can lead to nothing!

I have thought up a horrible dream to impute to
Hrothgar.

Hrothgar speaks:

I have dreamt it again: standing suddenly still
In a thicket, among wet trees, stunned, minutely
Shuddering, hearing a wooden echo escape.
A mossy floor, almost colorless, disappears
In depths of rain among the tree shapes.
I am straining, tasting that echo a second longer.

If I can hold it . . . familiar if I can hold it . . .
A black tree with a double trunk—two trees
Grown into one—throws up its blurred branches.

The two trunks in their infinitesimal dance of growth
Have turned completely about one another, their join
A slowly twisted scar . . . that I recognize. . . .

A quick arc flashes sidewise in the air,
A heavy blade in flight. A wooden stroke:
Iron sinks in the gasping core.
                                    I will dream it again.

9

December, approaching the year's darkest night, and the only way of the dream is down and through it.

The trees are dead.

The days are an arrow in a dead man's chest.

Snowlight blinds me, heatless fire; pale, apocalyptic.

The creeks are frozen; the deer show their ribs.

I find dead wolves—a paw, a scraggly tail sticking up through snow.

The trees are dead, and only the deepest religion can break through time and believe they'll revive. Against the snow, black cuts on a white, white hand.

In the town, children go down on their backs in the drifted snow and move their arms and, when they rise, leave behind them impressions, mysterious and ominous, of winged creatures. I come upon them as I move through sleeping streets to the meadhall, and though I know what they are, I pause and study them, picking at my lip.

I do not pretend to understand these feelings. I

record them, check them off one by one for the
dead ears of night.
Something is coming, strange as spring.
I am afraid.
Standing on an open hill, I imagine muffled foot-
steps overhead.

I watch one of Hrothgar's bowmen pursue a hart.
The man, furred from his toes to his ears, walks
through the moon-and-snowlit woods, silent as an
owl, huge bow on his shoulder, his eyes on the
dark tracks. He moves up a thickly wooded hill,
and at the crest of it, standing as if waiting for
him, he finds the hart. The antlers reach out, motionless, as still as the treelimbs overhead or the
stars above the trees. They're like wings, filled
with otherworldly light. Neither the hart nor the
hunter moves. Time is inside them, transferred
from chamber to chamber like sand in an hour-
glass; it can no more get outside than sand in the
lower chamber can rise to the upper without a hand
to turn stiff nature on its head. They face each
other, unmoving as numbers on a stick. And then,
incredibly, through the pale, strange light the man's
hand moves—click click click click—toward the
bow, and grasps it, and draws it down, away from
the shoulder and around in front (click click) and
transfers the bow to the slowly moving second
hand, and the first hand goes back up and (click)
over the shoulder and returns with an arrow, threads
the bow. Suddenly time is a rush for the hart: his
head flicks, he jerks, his front legs buckling, and
he's dead. He lies as still as the snow hurtling outward around him to the hushed world's rim.

The image clings to my mind like a growth. I sense some riddle in it.

Near Hrothgar's hall stand the images of the Scyldings' gods, grotesque faces carved out of wood or hacked from stone and set up in a circle, eyes staring inward, gazing thoughtfully at nothing. The priests approach them, carrying torches, their shaggy white heads bent, obsequious. "Great spirit," the chief of the priests wails, "ghostly Destroyer, defend the people of Scyld and kill their enemy, the terrible world-rim-walker!" I smile, arms folded on my chest, and wait, but nobody comes to kill me. They sing, an antique language as ragged and strange as their beards, a language closer to mine than to their own. They march in a circle, from god to god—maybe uncertain which one is the Great Destroyer. "Is it you?" their meek old faces ask, lifting the torch to each monster-shape in turn. "Not I," whispers the head with four eyes. "Not I," whispers sly old dagger-tooth. "Not I," says the wolf-god, the bull-god, the horse-god, the happily smiling god with the nose like a pig's. They stab a calf and burn it, the corpse still jerking. The old peasant, friend of Prince Hrothulf, whispers crossly: "In the old days they used to kill virgins. Religion is sick."

Which is true. There is no conviction in the old priests' songs; there is only showmanship. No one in the kingdom is convinced that the gods have life in them. The weak observe the rituals—take their hats off, put them on again, raise their arms, lower their arms, moan, intone, press their palms together —but no one harbors unreasonable expectations.

The strong—old Hrothgar, Unferth—ignore the images. The will to power resides among the stalactites of the heart. (Her-kapf.)

Once, years ago, for no particular reason, I wrecked the place; broke up the wooden gods like kindling and toppled the gods of stone. When they came out in the morning and saw what I'd done, no one was especially bothered except the priests. They lamented and tore their hair, the priests, as fraught and rhetorical as they were when they prayed, and after a few days their outcries made people uneasy. On the chance that there might be something to it all, whatever a reasonable man might think, the people tipped the stone gods up again, with levers and ropes, and began to carve new gods of wood to replace those I'd ruined. It was dull work, you could see by their faces, but it was, for some reason, necessary. When the ring was complete, I considered wrecking it again, but the gods were inoffensive, dull. I decided the hell with it.

I have eaten several priests. They sit on the stomach like duck eggs.

Midnight. I sit in the center of the ring of gods, musing on them, pursuing some thought that I cannot make come clear. They wait, as quiet as upright bones in the softly falling snow. So Hrothgar waits, lying on his back with his eyes open. Wealtheow lies on her back beside him, her eyes open, her hand resting lightly in his. Hrothulf's breathing changes. He is having bad dreams. Unferth sleeps fitfully, guarding the meadhall; and the Shaper, in his big house, tosses and turns. He has a fever. He mumbles a few inchoate phrases to someone who is not there. All the gods have hats of snow and snow-crested noses. In the town below me there are no lights left. Overhead, the stars are blanked out by clouds.

But someone is awake. I hear him coming toward me in the snow, vaguely alarming, approaching like an arrow in a slowed-down universe, and a shudder runs through me. Then I see him, and I laugh at my fear. An old priest, palsied, walking with a cane of ash. He thinks it has magic in it. "Who's there?" he pipes, coming to the edge of the ring. He has a black robe, and his beard, as white as the snow all around us, hangs almost to his knees. "Who's there?" he says again, and pokes himself through between two gods, feeling ahead of himself with the cane. "Is there somebody here?" he whimpers.

"It is I," I say. "The Destroyer."

A violent shock goes through him. He shakes all over, practically falls down. "My lord!" he whimpers. He goes down on his knees. "O blessed, blessed lord!" A look of doubt crosses his face, but he resists it. "I heard someone down here," he says. "I thought it was—" The doubt comes again, mixed with fear this time. He squints, cocks his head, struggling to penetrate his blindness by force of will. "I am Ork," he says uncertainly, "eldest and wisest of the priests." I smile, say nothing. I intend to paint the images with the old man's steaming blood. "I know all mysteries," the priest says. "I am the only man still living who has thought them all out."

"We are pleased with you, Ork," I say, voice very solemn. Then, suddenly impish—at times I cannot resist these things: "Tell us what you know of the King of the Gods."

"The King?" he says.

"The King." I do not giggle.

He rolls his blind eyes, figuring the odds, snatching through his mind for doctrines.

"Speak to us concerning His unspeakable beauty and danger," I say, and wait.

The snow falls softly on the images. The old priest, kneeling, has one knee on his beard and is unable to lift his head. He shakes all over, as if the palsy is something outside him, an element like wind.

"The King of Gods," he whispers, and searches his wits.

At last he folds his arthritic white hands, raises them before him like a nightmare flower, and speaks. "The King of Gods is the ultimate limitation," he keens, "and His existence is the ultimate irrationality." A tic goes down one cheek; jerks the corner of his mouth. "For no reason can be given for just that limitation which it stands in His nature to impose. The King of Gods is not concrete, but He is the ground for concrete actuality. No reason can be given for the nature of God, because that nature is the ground of rationality."

He tips his head, waiting for some response from me that will tell him how he's doing. I say nothing. The old man clears his throat, and his face takes on an expression still more holy. The tic comes again.

"The King of the Gods is the actual entity in virtue of which the entire multiplicity of eternal objects obtains its graded relevance to each stage of concrescence. Apart from Him, there can be no relevant novelty."

I notice, with surprise, that the priest's blind eyes are brimming with tears. They seep down his cheeks into his beard. I raise my fingers to my mouth, baffled.

"The Chief God's purpose in the creative advance is the evocation of novel intensities. He is the *lure for our feeling*." Ork is now weeping profusely, so moved that his throat constricts. I observe in wonder. His knotted hands shake and sway.

"He is the eternal urge of desire establishing the purposes of all creatures. He is an infinite patience, a tender care that nothing in the universe be vain."

He begins to moan, shaking violently, and it occurs to me that perhaps he is merely cold. But instead of hugging himself, as I expect him to, he stretches out his arms toward the sky, huge-knuckled fingers gnarled and twisted as if to frighten me. "O the ultimate evil in the temporal world is deeper than any specific evil, such as hatred, or suffering, or death! The ultimate evil is that Time is perpetual perishing, and being actual involves elimination. The nature of evil may be epitomized, therefore, in two simple but horrible and holy propositions: 'Things fade' and 'Alternatives exclude.' Such is His mystery: that beauty requires contrast, and that discord is fundamental to the creation of new intensities of feeling. Ultimate wisdom, I have come to perceive, lies in the perception that the solemnity and grandeur of the universe rise through the slow process of unification in which the diversities of existence are utilized, and nothing, *nothing* is lost." The old man falls forward, arms thrown out in front of him, and weeps with gratitude. I have trouble deciding what to do.

Before I can make up my mind about him, I

become aware that there are others moving toward the place, drawn by the old man's keening. So quietly that even old Ork cannot hear me, I tiptoe out of the ring and hide behind a fat stone image of a god with a skull in his lap and a blacksmith's apron. Three of his fellow priests arrive. They gather around him, bend over to look at him. The snow falls on them softly.

FIRST PRIEST: Ork, what are you doing here? It is written that the old shall keep to the comfort of their beds!

SECOND PRIEST: It's a bad habit, beloved friend, this wandering about at night when monsters prowl.

THIRD PRIEST: Senility. I've been telling you the old fool's gone senile.

ORK: Brothers, I've talked with the Great Destroyer!

THIRD PRIEST: Bosh.

FIRST PRIEST: Blasphemy! It is written: "Ye shall not see my face."

SECOND PRIEST: Think what shape you'll be in for your morning devotions!

ORK: He stood as near to me as you are.

FIRST PRIEST: "Worship is the work of priests. What the gods do is the business of the gods." You know the text.

THIRD PRIEST: He's a blamed fool. If a man hankers for visions, he should do it in public, where it does us some good.

SECOND PRIEST: It doesn't look right, beloved friend, wandering around in the middle of the night. A man should try to be more regular.

ORK: Nevertheless, I saw him. My life of study and devotion has been rewarded! I told him my opinion of the King of the Gods, and he didn't deny it. I believe I'm approximately right.

FIRST PRIEST: The theory's ridiculous. Idle speculation. For it is written—

SECOND PRIEST: Please do come in with us, beloved friend. I hate being up after midnight. It ruins me the whole next day. It makes me put my clothes on wrong, and scramble the service, and eat incorrectly—

THIRD PRIEST: Lunatic priests are bad business. They give people the willies. One man like him can turn us all to paupers.

As I listen, shaking my head at the strangeness of the priestly conversation, another priest comes running up, younger than the others, pulling his outer robe on as he comes. They turn their heads, looking at the younger priest in annoyance. It occurs to me that perhaps he has been drinking. "What's this?" he cries. "Precious gods, what's this?" He throws his hands out, delighted by all he sees. Ork tells him what he has seen, and he listens in rapture. Before Ork has finished, the younger priest drops to his knees and throws his hands up, shaggy lips smiling, wild.

FOURTH PRIEST: Blessed! O blessed! (On his knees he goes over to Ork, seizes the old man's head between his hands, and kisses him.) I feared for you, dear blessed Ork—I feared your bloodless rationalism. But now I see, I see! The will of the gods! The rhythm is re-established! Merely rational thought—forgive me for preaching, but I must, I must!—merely rational thought leaves the mind incurably crippled in a closed and ossified system, it can only extrapolate from the past. But now at last, sweet fantasy has found root in your blessed soul! The absurd, the inspiring, the uncanny, the awesome, the terrifying, the ecstatic—none of these had a place, for you, before. But I should have seen it coming. O I *kick* myself for not seeing it coming! A vision of the Destroyer! Of course, of course! Before we know it, you'll be kissing girls! Can't you grasp it, brothers? Both blood and sperm are explosive, irregular, feeling-pitched, messy—and inexplicably fascinating! They transcend! They leap the gap! O blessed Ork! I believe your vision proves there is hope for us all!

So he raves, overflowing with meadbowl joy, and the older three priests look down at him as they would at a wounded snake. Ork ignores him, sniffling privately. I back away. Even a monster's blood-lust can be stifled by such talk. They remain inside the image ring, snow falling softly on their hair and beards, and except for their forms, their prattle, the town is dead.

Hrothgar is asleep now, resting up for tomorrow's ordeal of waiting. Wealtheow breathes evenly, beside him. Hrothulf and the king's two children are asleep. In the main hall, row on row in their wall-hung beds, the guardians snore, except Unferth. Puffy-eyed, he gets up, and in a kind of stupor goes to the meadhall door to piss. A dog barks—not at me: I have put my spell on them. Unferth hardly hears. He looks out over the snowy rooftops of the town to the snowy moor, the snowy woods, unaware of my presence behind the wall.

The snow falls softly through the trees, closing up the foxes' dens, burying the tracks of sleeping deer. A wolf, asleep with his head on his paws, awakens at the sound of my footsteps and opens his eyes but does not lift his head. He watches me pass, his gray eyes hostile, then sleeps again, his cave half hidden by snow.

I do not usually raid in the winter, when the world is a corpse. I would be wiser to be curled up, asleep like a bear, in my cave. My heart moves slowly, like freezing water, and I cannot clearly recall the smell of blood. And yet I am restless. I would fall, if I could, through time and space to the dragon. I cannot. I walk slowly, wiping the snow from my face with the back of my arm. There is no sound on earth but the whispering snowfall. I recall something. A void boundless as a nether sky. I hang by the twisted roots of an oak, looking down into immensity. Vastly far away I see the sun, black but shining, and slowly revolving around it there are spiders. I pause in my tracks, puzzled—though not stirred—by what I see. But then I am in the woods again, and the snow is falling, and everything alive is fast asleep. It is just some dream. I move on, uneasy; waiting.

10

Tedium is the worst pain.

The dull victim, staring, vague-eyed, at seasons that never were meant to be observed.

The sun walks mindlessly overhead, the shadows lengthen and shorten as if by plan.

"The gods made this world for our joy!" the young priest squeals. The people listen to him dutifully, heads bowed. It does not impress them, one way or the other, that he's crazy.

The scent of the dragon is a staleness on the earth.

The Shaper is sick.

I watch a great horned goat ascend the rocks toward my mere. I have half a mind to admire his bottomless stupidity. "Hey, goat!" I yell down.

"There's nothing here. Go back." He lifts his head, considers me, then lowers it again to keep an eye on crevasses and seams, icy scree, slick rocky ledges—doggedly continuing. I tip up a boulder and let it fall thundering toward him. His ears flap up in alarm, he stiffens, looks around him in haste, and jumps. The boulder bounds past him. He watches it fall, then turns his head, looks up at me disapprovingly. Then, lowering his head again, he continues. It is the business of goats to climb. He means to climb. "Ah, goat, goat!" I say as if deeply disappointed in him. "Use your reason! There's nothing here!" He keeps on coming. I am suddenly annoyed, no longer amused by his stupidity. The mere belongs to me and the firesnakes. What if everybody should decide the place is public? "Go back down, goat!" I yell at him. He keeps on climbing, mindless, mechanical, because it is the business of goats to climb. "Not here," I yell. "If climbing's your duty to the gods, go climb the meadhall." He keeps on climbing. I run back from the edge to a dead tree, throw myself against it and break it off and drag it back to the cliffwall. "You've had fair warning," I yell at him. I'm enraged now. The words come echoing back to me. I lay the tree sideways, wait for the goat to be in better range, then shove. It drops with a crash and rolls crookedly toward him. He darts left, reverses himself and bounds to the right, and a limb catches him. He bleats, falling, flopping over with a jerk too quick for the eye, and bleats again, scrambling, sliding toward the ledge-side. The tree, slowly rolling, drops out of sight. His sharp front hooves dig in and he jerks to his feet, but before his balance is sure my stone hits him and falls again. I leap down to make certain he goes over this time. He finds his feet the same instant that my second stone hits. It splits his skull, and blood sprays out past his dangling brains, yet he doesn't fall. He threatens me, blind. It's not easy to kill a mountain goat. He thinks with his spine. A death tremor shakes his flanks, but he picks toward me, jerking his great twisted horns at air. I back off, upward toward the mere the goat will never reach. I smile, threatened by an animal already dead, still climbing. I snatch up a stone and hurl it. It smashes his mouth, spraying out teeth, and penetrates to the jugular. He drops to his knees, gets up again. The air is sweet with the scent of his blood. Death shakes his body the way high wind shakes trees. He climbs toward me. I snatch up a stone.

At dusk I watch men go about their business in the towns of the Scyldings. Boys and dogs drive the horses and oxen to the river and break through the ice to let them drink. Back at the barns, men carry in hay on wooden forks, dump grain in the mangers, and carry out manure. A wheelwright and his helper squat in their dark room hammering spokes into a hub. I listen to the grunt, the blow of the hammer, the grunt, the blow, like the sound of a leaky heart. Smells of cooking. Gray wood-smoke rises slowly toward a lead-gray sky. On the rocky cliffs looking out to sea, Hrothgar's watchmen, each man posted several stone's-throws away from the next, sit huddled in furs, on their horses' backs, or stand in the shelter of an out-cropping ledge, rubbing their hands together, stamping their feet. No one will strike at the kingdom from the sea: icebergs drift a mile out, grinding against one another from time to time, letting out a low moan like the sign of some huge sea-beast. The guards watch anyway, obedient to orders the king has forgotten to cancel.

People eat, leaning over their food together, seldom talking. The lamp at the center of the table lights their eyes. Dogs beside the men's legs wait, looking up from time to time, and the girl who brings the food from the stove stands looking at the wall as she waits for the plates to empty. An old man, finished before the rest, goes out to bring in wood. I spy on an old woman telling lies to children. (Her face is dark with some disease, and the veins on the backs of her hands are ropes. She is too old to sweep or cook.) She tells of a giant across the sea who has the strength of thirty thanes. "Someday he will come here," she tells the children. Their eyes widen. A bald old man looks up from his earthernware plate and laughs. A gray dog pushes against his leg. He kicks it.

The sun stays longer each day now, climbing mechanical as a goat off the leaden horizon. Children slide down the hills on shaped boards, sending their happy cries through drifted stillness. As twilight deepens, their mothers call them in. A few feign deafness. A shadow looms over them (mine) and they're gone forever.

So it goes.

Darkness. At the house of the Shaper, people come and go, solemn faced, treading softly, their heads bowed and their hands folded for fear of sending dreadful apparitions through his dreams. His attendant, the boy who came here with him—a grown man now—sits by the old man's bed and plays pale runs on the old man's harp. The old man turns his blind head, rising from confusion to listen. He asks about a certain woman who does not come. No answer.

But the king comes, with the queen on his arm, young Hrothulf walking four steps behind them, holding the hands of their children. The king sits beside the Shaper's bed as he sits in the hall, motionless, his patient eyes staring. Hrothulf and the children wait out in the entry room. The queen puts her fingertips gently on the old man's forehead.

The Shaper whispers for the lamp. The attendant pretends to bring it, though it stands already on the table beside his bed. "That's better," the queen says dutifully, and the king says, as if he couldn't see well before, "You look healthier today." The Shaper says nothing. Crouched in the bushes beside the path, peeking in like a whiskered old voyeur, wet-lipped, red-eyed, my chest filled with some meaningless anguish, I watch the old man working up the nerve to let his heart stop. "Where are all his fine phrases now?" I whisper to the night. I chuckle. The night, as usual, doesn't comment.

He sits motionless, propped up in bed, death-white hands folded on top of the covers: his eyes, once webbed with visions, are shut. The young man, the attendant sitting with the harp, does not play. The king and queen wait, dutiful, probably counting the time off in their heads, and the herbalist—humpbacked, robed in black (a tic screws taut one whole side of his face)—the herbalist, no longer useful to the onetime king of poets.

paces back and forth slowly, rubbing his hands. He waits for the soft, dry throat-rattle that will free him to go pace elsewhere.

The Shaper speaks. They bend closer. "I see a time," he says, "when the Danes once again—" His voice trails off; puzzlement crosses his forehead, and one hand reaches up feebly as if to smooth it away but forgets before it can find the forehead, and falls back to the covers. He lifts his head a little, listening for footsteps. There are none. The head drops back weakly. His visitors wait on. They do not seem to realize that he is dead.

In another house, at a large, carved table, a middle-aged woman with hair just slightly less red than the queen's (she has close-together eyes and eyebrows plucked neat as the lines of a knife wound) sits by lamplight listening, as he did, for footsteps. Her nobleman husband lies sleeping in a nearby room, his head on his arm, as if listening to his heartbeat. She is a lady I have watched with the greatest admiration. Soul of fidelity, decorum. The Shaper would tip his whitened head, blind eyes staring at the floor whenever the lady spoke, and from time to time, when he sang of heroes, of ship-backs broken, there was no mistaking that he sang the song for her. Nothing came of it. She would leave the hall on her husband's arm: the Shaper would bow politely as she passed.

She hears them coming. I duck into the gloom to watch and wait. The messenger the Shaper's attendant has sent goes up to the door and has hardly knocked once when the door opens inward and the lady appears, staring through him. "He's dead," says the messenger. The lady nods. When the messenger is gone, the lady comes out onto the steps and stands with her arms locked, expressionless. She looks up the hill toward the meadhall.

"So all of us must sooner or later pass," I am tempted to whisper. "Alas! Woe!" I resist.

Only the wind is alive, pressing her robe to her fat, loose hips and bosom. The woman is as still as the dead man in his bed. I am tempted to snatch her. How her squeals would dance on the icicle-walls of the night! But I back away. I look in on the Shaper one more time. The old women are arranging him, putting gold coins on his eyelids to preserve him from seeing where he goes. At last, unsatisfied as ever, I slink back home.

In my cave the tedium is worse, of course. My mother no longer shows any sign of sanity, hurrying back and forth, wall to wall, sometimes on two legs, sometimes on four, dark forehead furrowed like a new-plowed field, her eyes glittering and crazy as a captured eagle's. Each time I come in she gets between me and the door, as if to lock me up with her forever. I endure it, for the time. When I sleep, she presses close to me, half buries me under her thistly fur and fat. "Dool-dool," she moans. She drools and weeps. "Warovvish," she whimpers, and tears at herself. Hanks of fur come away in her claws. I see gray hide. I study her, cool and objective in my corner, and because now the Shaper is dead, strange thoughts come over me. I think of the pastness of the past: how the moment I am alive in, prisoned in, moves like a slowly tumbling form through darkness, the underground river. Not only ancient history—the mythical age of the brothers' feud—but my own history one second ago, has vanished utterly, dropped out of existence. King Scyld's great deeds do not exist "back there" in Time. "Back there in Time" is an allusion of language. They do not exist at all. My wickedness five years ago, or six, or twelve, has no existence except as now, mumbling, mumbling, sacrificing the slain world to the omnipotence of words, I strain my memory to regain it. I snatch by my wits a time when I was very small amd my mama held me softly in her arms. Ah, ah, how I loved you, Mama—dead these many years! I snatch a time when I crouched outside the meadhall hearing the first strange hymns of the Shaper. Beauty! Holiness! How my heart rocked! He is dead. I should have captured him, teased him, tormented him, made a fool of him. I should have cracked his skull midsong and sent his blood spraying out wet through the meadhall like a shocking change of key. One evil deed missed is a loss for all eternity.

I decide, naturally, to attend his funeral. She tries to prevent me. I lift her by the armpits as though she were a child and, gently, I set her aside. Her face trembles, torn, I think, between terror and self-pity. It crosses my mind that she knows something, but she doesn't, I know. The future is as dark, as unreal, as the past. Coolly, objectively, I watch the trembling; it's as if all the muscles are locked to the charge of an eel. Then I push her away. The face shatters, she whoops. I run to the pool and dive, and even now I can hear her. I will forget, tomorrow, so her pain is a matter of indifference.

And so to the funeral.

The Shaper's assistant, cradling the old man's

polished harp, sings of Hoc and Hildeburh and
Hnaef and Hengest, how Finn's thanes fought
with his wife's dear kinsmen and killed King
Hnaef, and a terrible thing ensued. When Finn had
few men and his enemies had no king, they
made a truce, and the terms were these: that Finn
would be lord of the lordless Danes, because a
king without men is a worthless thing, and thanes
without a lord are exiles. Both sides made vows,
swore the duty of peace, and so winter came, in
its time, to the country of the Jutes.

The people listen silent and solemn to the old
Shaper's song on the young man's lips, and the
pyre where the old man lies stands waiting for
fire. The dead arms are crossed, the features are
stiff and blue, as if frozen. Ice glints on the sides
of the pyre. The world is white.

>   *Young Hengest still*
> *through slaughter-dark winter stayed with Finn,*
> *heart sorrowing. He thought of home,*
> *though he could not drive on the dark sea*
> *his ring-prowed ship; for the sea-air rolled,*
> *dusky with wind, and the waves were locked*
> *in ice. Then another season came,*
> *another year, as the years do yet,*
> *bright shining weather awaiting its time.*
> *The winter was gone, earth's breast was fair,*
> *and the exiled Hengest was eager to go,*
> *unwilling guest from the dwelling.—Yet as*
> *ice-chains locked the land, so Hengest's heart*
> *was locked: revenge called harder to him than home.*
> *He cried in his mind for quarrel, and quarrel came.*
> *Then Finn lay down in blood, bold king*
> *with all his company, and the queen was taken;*
> *and, loaded with rings King Finn could not refuse,*
> *the Danes sailed home. Men's double vows*
> *soon wash away. Spring rain drips down through rafters.*

So he sings, looking down, recalling and repeating the words, hands light on the harp. The king listens, dry-eyed, his mind far, far away. Prince Hrothulf stands with the children of Hrothgar and Wealtheow, his features revealing no more secrets than does snow. Men light the pyre. Unferth stares at the flames with eyes like stones. I too watch the fire, as well as I can. Colorless it seems. A more intense place in the brightness of snow and ice. It flames high at once, as if hungry for the coarse, lean meat. The priests walk slowly around the pyre, saying antique prayers, and the crowd, all in black, ignoring the black priests, keens. I watch the burning head burst, bare of visions, dark blood dripping from the corner of the mouth and the ear.

End of an epoch, I could tell the king.

We're on our own again. Abandoned.

I awaken with a start and imagine I hear the goat still picking at the cliffwall, climbing to the mere. Something groans, far out at sea.

My mother makes sounds. I strain my wits toward them, clench my mind. *Beware the fish.*

I get up and walk, filled with restless expectation, though I know there is nothing to expect.

I am not the only monster on these moors.
I met an old woman as wild as the wind
Striding in white out of midnight's den.
Her cloak was in rags, and her flesh it was lean,
And her eyes, her murdered eyes . . .
Scent of the dragon.

I should sleep, drop war till spring as I normally do.

When I sleep I wake up in terror, with hands on my throat.

A stupid business.

Nihil ex nihilo, I always say.

11

I am mad with joy.—At least I think it's joy. Strangers have come, and it's a whole new game. I kiss the ice on the frozen creeks, I press my ear to it, honoring the water that rattles below, for by water they came: the icebergs parted as if gently pushed back by enormous hands, and the ship sailed through, sea-eager, foamy-necked, white sails riding the swan-road, flying like a bird! O happy Grendel! Fifteen glorious heroes, proud in their battle dress, fat as cows!

I could feel them coming as I lay in the dark of my cave. I stirred, baffled by the strange sensation, squinting into dark corners to learn the cause. It drew me as the mind of the dragon did once. *It's coming!* I said. More clearly than ever I heard the muffled footsteps on the dome of the world, and even when I realized that the footsteps were nothing but the sound of my own heart, I knew more surely than before that something was coming. I got up, moved past stone icicles to the pool and the sunken door. My mother made no move to prevent me. At the pool, firesnakes shot away from me

in all directions, bristling, hissing, mysteriously
wrought up. They had sensed it too. That beat—
steady, inhumanly steady; inexorable. And so, an
hour before dawn, I crouched in shadows at the
rocky sea-wall, foot of the giants' work. Low tide.
Lead-gray water sucked quietly, stubborn and de-
liberate, at icy gray boulders. Gray wind teased
leafless trees. There was no sound but the ice-cold
surge, the cry of a gannet, invisible in grayness
above me. A whale passed, long dark shadow two
miles out. The sky grew light at my back. Then I
saw the sail.

I was not the only one who saw them coming.
A lone Danish coastguard stood bundled in furs,
his horse beside him, and he shaded his eyes against
the glint of the icebergs beyond the sail and watched
the strangers come swiftly in toward land. The
wooden keel struck sand and cut a gouge toward
the boulders on the shore—a forty-foot cut, half
the length of the ship—and then, quick as wolves—
but mechanical, terrible—the strangers leaped
down, and with stiff, ice-crusted ropes as gray as
the sea, the sky, the stones, they moored their craft.
Their chain-mail rattled as they worked—never
speaking, walking dead men—lashing the helm-bar,
lowering the sail, unloading ashspear shafts and
battle-axes. The coastguard mounted, snatched up
his spear, and rode loudly down to meet them.
His horse's hooves shot sparks. I laughed. If they
were here for war, the coastguard was a goner.

"What are ye, bearers of armor, dressed in mail-
coats, that have thus come riding your tall ship
over the searoad, winter-cold ocean, here to Dane-
land?" Thus spake the coastguard. Wind took his
words and sent them tumbling.

I bent double, soundlessly laughing till I thought

I'd split. They were like trees, these strangers. Their leader was big as a mountain, moving with his forest toward the guard. Nevertheless, the Dane shook his spear the way attackers do when they're telling a man what they're going to do with his testicles. "Attaboy!" I whisper. I shadow box. "If they come at you, bite 'em in the leg!"

He scolded and fumed and demanded their lineage; they listened with folded arms. The wind blew colder. At last the coastguard's voice gave out—he bent over the pommel, coughing into his fist—and the leader answered. His voice, though powerful, was mild. Voice of a dead thing, calm as dry sticks and ice when the wind blows over them. He had a strange face that, little by little grew unsettling to me: it was a face, or so it seemed for an instant, from a dream I had almost forgotten. The eyes slanted downward, never blinking, unfeeling as a snake's. He had no more beard than a fish. He smiled as he spoke, but it was as if the gentle voice, the childlike yet faintly ironic smile were holding something back, some magician-power that could blast stone cliffs to ashes as lightning blasts trees.

"We're Geats," he said, "the hearth-companions of King Hygilac. You've heard of my father. A famous old man named Ecgtheow." His mind, as he spoke, seemed far away, as if, though polite, he were indifferent to all this—an outsider not only among the Danes but everywhere. He said: "We've come as friends for a visit with your lord King Hrothgar, protector of the people." He tipped his head, pausing. You'd have thought he had centuries. At last with a little shrug, he said, "Be so kind as to give us some advice, old man. We've come on a fairly important errand." The hint of irony in the smile grew darker, and he looked now not at the coastguard but at the coastguard's horse. "A certain thing can't very well be kept hidden, I think. You'll know if it's true, as we heard back home, that I don't know what kind of enemy stalks your hall at night—kills men, so they say, and for some reason scorns your warriors. If it's so—" He paused, his eyebrows cocked, and glanced at the coastguard and smiled, "I've come to give Hrothgar advice."

You could see pretty well what advice he'd give. His chest was as wide as an oven. His arms were like beams. "Come ahead," I whispered. "Make your play. Do your worst." But I was less sure of myself than I pretended. Staring at his grotesquely muscled shoulders—stooped, naked despite the cold, sleek as the belly of a shark and as rippled with power as the shoulders of a horse—I found my mind wandering. If I let myself, I could drop into a trance just looking at those shoulders. He was dangerous. And yet I was excited, suddenly alive. He talked on. I found myself not listening, merely looking at his mouth, which moved—or so it seemed to me—independent of the words, as if the body of the stranger were a ruse, a disguise for something infinitely more terrible. Then the coastguard turned his horse and led them up to where the stone-paved road began, gray as the sea, between snowbanks. "I'll have men guard your ship," he said. He pointed out the meadhall, high on its hill above the town. Then he turned back. The sea-pale eyes of the stranger were focused on nothing. He and his company went on, their weapons clinking, chain-mail jangling, solemn and ominous as drums. They moved like one creature, huge strange machine. Sunlight gleamed on their helmets and cheekguards and flashed off their spearpoints, blinding. I did not follow. I stayed in the ruin, prowling where long-dead giants prowled, my heart aching to know what the strangers were doing now, up at the meadhall. But it was daylight; I'd be a fool to go up and see.

I couldn't tell, back in my cave, whether I was afraid of them or not. My head ached from staying too long in the sunlight, and my hands had no grip. It was as if they were asleep. I was unnaturally conscious, for some reason, of the sounds in the cave: the roar of the underground river hundreds of feet below our rooms, reaming out walls, driving deeper and deeper; the centuries-old drip-drip of seepage building stalagmites, an inch in a hundred years; the spatter of the spring three rooms away —the room of the pictures half buried in stone— where the spring breaks through the roof. Half awake, half asleep, I felt as if I were myself the cave, my thoughts coursing downward through my own strange hollows . . . or some impulse older and darker than thought, as old as the mindless mechanics of a bear, the twilight meditations of a wolf, a tree . . .

Who knows what all this means? Neither awake nor asleep, my chest filled with an excitement like joy, I tried to think whether or not I was afraid of the strangers, and the thought made no sense. It was unreal—insubstantial as spiderweb-strands blowing lightly across a window that looks out on trees. I have sometimes watched men do mysterious things. A man with a wife and seven children, a carpenter with a fair reputation as wise, not maddened by passions, not given to foolishness—regular of habit, dignified in bearing, a dedicated craftsman (no edge unbeveled, no ragged peg, no gouge or split) —once crept from his house at the edge of the town while his family slept, and fled down snowy paths through woods to the house of a hunter away in search of game. The hunter's wife admitted him, and he slept with her until the second rooster crowed then he fled back home. Who knows why? Tedium is the worst pain. The mind lays out the world in blocks, and the hushed blood waits for revenge. All order, I've come to understand, is theoretical, unreal—a harmless, sensible, smiling mask men slide between the two great, dark realities, the self and the world—two snake-pits. The watchful mind lies, cunning and swift, about the dark blood's lust, lies and lies and lies until, weary of talk, the watchman sleeps. Then sudden and swift the enemy strikes from nowhere, the cavernous heart. Violence is truth, as the crazy old peasant told Hrothulf. But the old fool only half grasped what he said. He had never conversed with a dragon. And the stranger?

Afraid or not, I would go to the meadhall, I knew. I toyed, of course, with the ridiculous theory that I'd stay where I was safe, like a sensible beast. "Am I not free?—as free as a bird?" I whispered, leering, maniacal. I have seen—I embody—the vision of the dragon: absolute, final waste. I saw long ago the whole universe as not-my-mother, and I glimpsed my place in it, a hole. *Yet I exist*, I knew. *Then I alone exist*, I said. *It's me or it*. What glee, that glorious recognition! (The cave my cave is a jealous cave.) For even my mama loves me not for myself, my holy specialness (he he ho ha), but for my son-ness, my possessedness, my displacement of air as visible proof of her power. I have set her aside—gently, picking her up by the armpits as I would a child—and so have proved that she has no power but the little I give her by momentary whim. So I might set aside Hrothgar's whole kingdom and all his thanes if I did not, for sweet desire's sake, set limits to desire. If I murdered the last of the Scyldings, what would I live for? I'd have to move.

So now, for once unsure of victory, I might set limits to desire: go to sleep, put off further raids till the Geats go home. For the world is divided, experience teaches, into two parts: things to be murdered, and things that would hinder the murder of things: and the Geats might reasonably be defined either way. So I whispered, wading through drifts waist-high, inexorably on my way to Hrothgar's meadhall. Darkness lay over the world like a coffin lid. I hurried. It would be a shame to miss the boasting. I came to the hall, bent down at my chink, peered in. The wind was shrill, full of patterns.

It was a scene to warm the cockles of your heart. The Danes were not pleased, to say the least, that the Geats had come to save them. Honor is very big with them; they'd rather be eaten alive than be bailed out by strangers. The priests weren't happy either. They'd been saying for years that the ghostly Destroyer would take care of things in time. Now here were these foreigner upstarts unmasking religion! My old friend Ork sat shaking his head in dismay, saying nothing, brooding, no doubt, on the dark metaphysical implications. Things fade; alternatives exclude. Whichever of us might exclude the other, when the time came for me and the stranger to meet, the eyes of the people would be drawn to the instance, they would fail to rise to the holy idea of process. Theology does not thrive in the world of action and reaction, change: it grows on calm, like the scum on a stagnant pool. And it flourishes, it prospers, on decline. Only in a world where everything is patently being lost can a priest stir men's hearts as a poet would by maintaining that nothing is in vain. For old times' sake, for the old priest's honor, I would have to kill the stranger. And for the honor of Hrothgar's thanes.

The Danes sat sulking, watching the strangers eat, wishing some one of them would give them an excuse to use their daggers. I covered my mouth to keep from cackling. The king presided, solemn and irritable. He knew that his thanes couldn't handle me alone, and he was too old and tired to be much impressed—however useful it might be to his kingdom—by their fathead ideas of honor. *Get through the meal, that's the thing,* he was thinking. *Keep them from wasting their much touted skills on one another.* The queen wasn't present. Situation much too touchy.

Then up spoke Unferth, Ecglaf's son, top man in Hrothgar's hall. He had a nose like a black, deformed potato, eyes like a couple of fangs. He leaned forward over the table and pointed the dagger he'd been eating with. "Say, friend," he said to the beardless leader of the Geats, "are you the same man that went swimming that time with young Breca—risked your lives in the middle of the winter for nothing—for a crazy meadboast?"

The stranger stopped eating, smiled.

"We heard about that," Unferth said. "Nobody could stop you—kings, priests, councilors—nobody. Splash! *Uh, uh, uh!*" Unferth made swimming motions, eyes rolled up, mouth gasping. The thanes around him laughed. "The sea boiled with waves, fierce winter swells. Seven nights you swam, so people say." He made his face credulous, and the Danes laughed again. "And at last Breca beat you, much stronger than you were. He proved his boast against you—for what it may be worth." The Danish thanes laughed. Even Hrothgar smiled. Unferth grew serious, and now only the stranger went on smiling, he alone and the huge Geats next to him, patient as timberwolves. Unferth pointed with his dagger, giving friendly advice. "I predict it will go even worse for you tonight. You may have had successes—I haven't heard. But wait up for Grendel for one night's space and all your glorious successes will be done with."

The Danes applauded. The stranger smiled on, his downward-slanting eyes like empty pits. I could see his mind working, stone-cold, grinding like a millwheel. When the hall was still, he spoke, soft-voiced, his weird gaze focused nowhere. "Ah, friend Unferth, drunk with mead you've said a good deal about Breca. The truth is, nevertheless, that I beat him. I'm stronger in the ocean than any other man alive. Like foolish boys we agreed on the match and boasted, yes . . . we were both very young . . . swore we'd risk our lives in the sea, and did so. We took swords with us, swimming one-handed, to fight off whales."

Unferth laughed, and the others followed, as was right. It was preposterous.

The stranger said, "Breca couldn't swim away from me, for all his strength—a man with arms like yours, friend Unferth—and as for myself, I chose not to swim away from him. Thus we swam for five nights, and then a storm came up, icy wind from the north, black sky, raging waves, and we were separated. The turmoil stirred up the sea-monsters. One of them attacked me, dragged me down to the bottom where the weight of the sea would have crushed any other man. But it was granted to me that I might kill him with my sword, which same I did. Then others attacked. They pressed me hard. I killed them, nine old water nickers, robbed them of the feast they expected at the bottom of the sea. In the morning, sword-ripped, they lay belly-up near shore. They'd trouble no more passing sailors after that. Light came from the east and, behold, I saw headlands, and I swam to them. Fate often enough will spare a man if his courage holds."

Now the Danes weren't laughing. The stranger said it all so calmly, so softly, that it was impossible to laugh. He believed every word he said. I understood at last the look in his eyes. He was insane.

Even so, I wasn't prepared for what came next. Nobody was. Solemn, humorless despite the slightly ironic smile, he suddenly cut deep—yet with the same mildness, the same almost inhuman indifference except for the pale flash of fire in his eyes. "Neither Breca nor you ever fought such battles," he said. "I don't boast much of that. Nevertheless, I don't recall hearing any glorious deeds of yours, except that you murdered your brothers. You'll prowl the stalagmites of hell for that, friend Unferth—clever though you are."

The hall was numb. The stranger was no player of games.

And yet he was shrewd, you had to grant. Whether or not they believed his wild tale of superhuman strength, no thane in the hall would attack him again and risk the slash of that mild, coolly murderous tongue.

Old King Hrothgar, for one, was pleased. The madman's single-mindedness would be useful in a monster fight. He spoke: "Where's the queen?

We're all friends in this hall! Let her come to us and pass the bowl!"

She must have been listening behind her door. She came out, radiant, and crossed swiftly to the great golden bowl on the table by the hearth. As if she'd brought light and warmth with her, men began talking, joking, laughing, both Danes and Geats together. When she'd served all the Danes and the lesser Geats, she stood, red hair flowing, her neck and arms adorned in gold, by the leader of the strangers. "I thank God," she said, "that my wish has been granted, that at last I have found a man whose courage I can trust."

The stranger smiled, glanced at Unferth. Hrothgar's top man had recovered a little, though his neck was still dark red.

"We'll see," the stranger said.

And again I found something peculiar happening to my mind. His mouth did not seem to move with his words, and the harder I stared at his gleaming shoulders, the more uncertain I was of their shape. The room was full of a heavy, unpleasant scent I couldn't place. I labor to remember something: twisted roots, an abyss . . . I lose it. The queer little spasm of terror passes. Except for his curious beardlessness, there is nothing frightening about the stranger. I've broken the backs of bulls no weaker than he is.

Hrothgar made speeches, his hand on the queen's. Unferth sat perfectly still, no longer blushing. He was struggling to make himself hope for the stranger's success, no doubt. *Heroism is more than noble language, dignity. Inner heroism, that's the trick! Glorious carbuncle of the soul! Except in the life of the hero the whole world's meaningless.* He took a deep breath. He would try to be a better person, yes. He forced a smile, but it twisted, out of his control. Tears! He got up suddenly and, without a word, walked out.

Hrothgar told the hall that the stranger was like a son to him. The queen's smile was distant, and the nephew, Hrothulf, picked at the table with a dirty fingernail. "You already have more sons than you need," the queen laughed lightly. Hrothgar laughed too, though he didn't seem to get it. He was tipsy. The stranger went on sitting with the same unlighted smile. The old king chatted of his plans for Freawaru, how he would marry her off to his enemy, the king of the Heathobards. The stranger smiled on, but closed his eyes. He knew a doomed house when he saw it, I had a feeling; but for one reason or another he kept his peace. I grew more and more afraid of him and at the same time—who can explain it?—more and more eager for the hour of our meeting.

The queen rose, at last, and retired. The fire in the hearth had now died down. The priests filed out to the god-ring to do their devotions. Nobody followed. I could hear them in the distance: "O ghostly Destroyer . . ." The cold ring of gods stared inward with large, dead eyes.

It is the business of rams to be rams and of goats to be goats, the business of shapers to sing and of kings to rule. The stranger waits on, as patient as a grave-mound. I too wait, whispering, whispering, mad like him. Time grows, obeying its mechanics, like all of us. So the young Shaper observes, singing to the few who remain, fingertips troubling a dead man's harp.

Frost shall freeze, and fire melt wood;
the earth shall give fruit, and ice shall bridge

dark water, make roofs, mysteriously lock
earth's flourishings; but the fetters of frost
shall also fall, fair weather return,
and the reaching sun restore the restless sea....

We wait.
The King retires, and his people leave.
The Geats build up the fire, prepare to sleep.
And now, silence.
Darkness.
It is time.

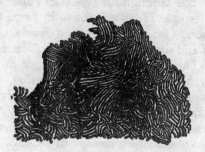

12

I touch the door with my fingertips and it bursts,
for all its fire-forged bands—it jumps away like a
terrified deer—and I plunge into the silent, hearth-
lit hall with a laugh that I wouldn't much care to
wake up to myself. I trample the planks that a
moment before protected the hall like a hand raised
in horror to a terrified mouth (sheer poetry, ah!)
and the broken hinges rattle like swords down the
timbered walls. The Geats are stones, and whether
it's because they're numb with terror or stiff from
too much mead, I cannot tell. I am swollen with
excitement, bloodlust and joy and a strange fear
that mingle in my chest like the twisting rage of
a bone-fire. I step onto the brightly shining floor
and angrily advance on them. They're all asleep,
the whole company! I can hardly believe my luck
and my wild heart laughs, but I let out no sound.
Swiftly, softly, I will move from bed to bed and
destroy them all, swallow every last man. I am
blazing, half-crazy with joy. For pure, mad
prank, I snatch a cloth from the nearest table and
tie it around my neck to make a napkin. I delay

no longer. I seize up a sleeping man, tear at him hungrily, bite through his bone-locks and suck hot, slippery blood. He goes down in huge morsels, head, chest, hips, legs, even the hands and feet. My face and arms are wet, matted. The napkin is sopping. The dark floor steams. I move on at once and I reach for another one (whispering, whispering, chewing the universe down to words), and I seize a wrist. A shock goes through me. Mistake!

It's a trick! His eyes are open, were open all the time, cold-bloodedly watching to see how I work. The eyes nail me now as his hand nails down my arm. I jump back without thinking (whispering wildly: *jump back without thinking*). Now he's out of his bed, his hand still closed like a dragon's jaws on mine. Nowhere on middle-earth, I realize, have I encountered a grip like his. My whole arm's on fire, incredible, searing pain—it's as if his crushing fingers are charged like fangs with poison. I scream, facing him, grotesquely shaking hands—dear long-lost brother, kinsman-thane—and the timbered hall screams back at me. I feel the bones go, ground from their sockets, and I scream again. I am suddenly awake. The long pale dream, my history, falls away. The meadhall is alive, great cavernous belly, gold-adorned, bloodstained, howling back at me, lit by the flickering fire in the stranger's eyes. He has wings. Is it possible? And yet it's true: out of his shoulders come terrible fiery wings. I jerk my head, trying to drive out illusion. The world is what it is and always was. That's our hope, our chance. Yet even in times of catastrophe we people it with tricks. Grendel, Grendel, hold fast to what is true!

Suddenly, darkness. My sanity has won. He's only

a man; I can escape him. I plan. I feel the plan
moving inside me like thaw-time waters rising
between cliffs. When I'm ready, I give a fero-
cious kick—but something's wrong: I am spinning—
Wa!—falling through bottomless space—*Wa!*—
snatching at the huge twisted roots of an oak . . .
a blinding flash of fire . . . no, darkness. I concen-
trate. I have fallen! Slipped on blood. He viciously
twists my arm behind my back. By accident, it
comes to me, I have given him a greater advantage.
I could laugh. *Woe, woe!*

And now something worse. He's whispering—
spilling words like showers of sleet, his mouth three
inches from my ear. I will not listen. I continue
whispering. As long as I whisper myself I need not
hear. His syllables lick at me, chilly fire. His syllables lick at me, chilly fire. His syllables lick at
me, chilly fire. His syllables lick . . .

*A meaningless swirl in the stream of time, a
temporary gathering of bits, a few random specks,
a cloud . . . Complexities: green dust, purple dust,
gold. Additional refinements: sensitive dust, copulating dust . . .*

The world is my bone-cave, I shall not want . . .
(He laughs as he whispers. I roll my eyes back.
Flames slip out at the corners of his mouth.) *As
you see it it is, while the seeing lasts, dark night-
mare-history, time-as-coffin; but where the water
was rigid there will be fish, and men will survive
on their flesh till spring. It's coming, my brother.
Believe it or not. Though you murder the world,
turn plains to stone, transmogrify life into I and it,
strong searching roots will crack your cave and
rain will cleanse it: The world will burn green,
sperm build again. My promise. Time is the mind,*

the hand that makes (fingers on harpstrings, hero-swords, the acts, the eyes of queens). By that I kill you.

I do not listen. I am sick at heart. I have been betrayed before by talk like that. "Mama!" I bawl. Shapes vague as lurking seaweed surround us. My vision clears. The stranger's companions encircle us, useless swords. I could laugh if it weren't for the pain that makes me howl. And yet I address him, whispering, whimpering, whining.

"If you win, it's by mindless chance. Make no mistake. First you tricked me, and then I slipped. Accident."

He answers with a twist that hurls me forward screaming. The thanes make way. I fall against a table and smash it, and wall timbers crack. And still he whispers.

Grendel, Grendel! You make the world by whispers, second by second. Are you blind to that? Whether you make it a grave or a garden of roses is not the point. Feel the wall: is it not hard? He smashes me against it, breaks open my forehead. *Hard, yes! Observe the hardness, write it down in careful runes. Now sing of walls! Sing!*

I howl.

Sing!

"I'm singing!"

Sing words! Sing raving hymns!

"You're crazy. Ow!"

Sing!

"I sing of walls," I howl. "Hooray for the hardness of walls!"

Terrible, he whispers. *Terrible.* He laughs and lets out fire.

"You're crazy," I say. "If you think I created that

wall that cracked my head, you're a fucking lunatic."

Sing walls, he hisses.

I have no choice.

"The wall will fall to the wind as the windy
   hill
will fall, and all things thought in former times:
Nothing made remains, nor man remembers.
And these towns shall be called the shining
   towns!"

Better, he whispers. *That's better*. He laughs again, and the nasty laugh admits I'm slyer than he guessed.

He's crazy. I understand him all right, make no mistake. Understand his lunatic theory of matter and mind, the chilly intellect, the hot imagination, blocks and builder, reality as stress. Nevertheless, it was by accident that he got my arm behind me. He penetrated no mysteries. He was lucky. If I'd known he was awake, if I'd known there was blood on the floor when I gave him that kick . . .

The room goes suddenly white, as if struck by lightning. I stare down, amazed. He has torn off my arm at the shoulder! Blood pours down where the limb was. I cry, I bawl like a baby. He stretches his blinding white wings and breathes out fire. I run for the door and through it. I move like wind. I stumble and fall, get up again. I'll die! I howl. The night is aflame with winged men. *No, no! Think!* I come suddenly awake once more from the nightmare. Darkness. I really will die! Every rock, every tree, every crystal of snow cries out cold-blooded objectness. Cold, sharp outlines, everything around me: distinct, detached as dead men. I understand. "Mama!" I bellow. "Mama, Mama! I'm dying!" But her love is history. His whispering follows me into the woods, though I've outrun him. "It was an accident," I bellow back. I will cling to what is true. "Blind, mindless, mechanical. Mere logic of chance." I am weak from loss of blood. No one follows me now. I stumble again and with my one weak arm I cling to the huge twisted roots of an oak. I look down past stars to a terrifying darkness. I seem to recognize the place, but it's impossible. "Accident," I whisper. I will fall. I seem to desire the fall, and though I fight it with all my will I know in advance that I can't win. Standing baffled, quaking with fear, three feet from the edge of a nightmare cliff, I find myself, incredibly, moving toward it. I look down, down, into bottomless blackness, feeling the dark power moving in me like an ocean current, some monster inside me, deep sea wonder, dread night monarch astir in his cave, moving me slowly to my voluntary tumble into death.

Again sight clears. I am slick with blood. I discover I no longer feel pain. Animals gather around me, enemies of old, to watch me die. I give them what I hope will appear a sheepish smile. My heart booms terror. Will the last of my life slide out if I let out breath? They watch with mindless, indifferent eyes, as calm and midnight black as the chasm below me.

Is it joy I feel?

They watch on, evil, incredibly stupid, enjoying my destruction.

"Poor Grendel's had an accident," I whisper. "*So may you all.*"

About the Author

JOHN GARDNER was accorded wide praise for his works of imagination, of criticism and of scholarship. He is the author of, among other books, *Grendel*, *The Sunlight Dialogues*, *Nickel Mountain*, *October Light*, *On Moral Fiction* and *The Art of Fiction*. Among the universities at which he taught are Oberlin, Northwestern, Southern Illinois, Bennington and the State University of New York–Binghamton. He was born in Batavia, New York, in 1933 and died in 1982.